I0831394

NO ONE SLEEPS ON THE ORIENT EXPRESS

IRENE HAGAN

VELVET KEY PRESS

Published by **Velvet Key Press**

Boston, Massachusetts

For the ones who haven't left — yet.

1

Turning fifty, Iris Quinn decided, was not what the brochure had promised.

Not that there had been a brochure.

But if there had been—if someone had handed her a glossy pamphlet at forty-five, outlining what to expect from this particular milestone—she felt certain it would have mentioned something. Fireworks, perhaps. Or clarity. Or at the very least, the quiet satisfaction of finally knowing where she kept her reading glasses.

Instead, she was in the library break room, eating grocery-store cake while her coworkers discussed Janet's new refrigerator.

"French doors," Janet was saying. "And the ice maker is inside the freezer, so you still get the full width of the shelves."

"That's the dream," Mrs. Henderson said, with surprising conviction.

Iris took a sip of coffee that had gone cold sometime during the ice-maker portion of the conversation. Around her, the discussion continued. Cubic footage, crisper drawer humidity settings, whether stainless steel showed fingerprints more than black. The enthusiasm was genuine. Maybe Mrs. Henderson was right.

Maybe the secret to happiness was wanting a refrigerator and then getting one.

"The old one still worked," Janet admitted. "But it was so dated."

Of course it still worked, Iris thought. That was never the point.

She looked from her coworkers to the cake, half-eaten on the counter. Vanilla on one side, chocolate on the other, even though her favorite was carrot cake. Not that anyone had asked. This was fifty. Not a crisis. Not a celebration. Just a Tuesday that happened to mark another year of showing up.

She scraped frosting off her fork and did the math.

Twenty-three years at this library. Twenty-three years of helping other people find what they were looking for. She was good at it—exceptionally so. She could find anything for anyone.

But somewhere along the way, she'd stopped looking for anything for herself.

She ate the cake. It was too sweet. But she ate it anyway, because that's what you did.

THE WALK HOME TOOK TWENTY MINUTES, MOST OF IT IN A DRIZZLE THAT couldn't quite commit to being rain. At intersections, crosswinds kept inverting her umbrella, each gust a small personal humiliation. The bakery had closed early, a handwritten sign in the window apologizing for "any inconvenience this may cause," as though inconvenience were a weather event—unpredictable, regrettable—rather than the direct result of someone locking the door.

Iris stepped over a deflated balloon on the sidewalk. Silver. PARTY still visible in sad block letters. She made a deliberate decision not to see it as a metaphor. Some things were just litter.

Her third floor apartment greeted her in the same way it always did. Without fanfare.

Beige walls she'd been meaning to paint for six years. A sofa that had started as a sensible, temporary choice and somehow lasted more than a decade, its cushions molded to her particular way of sitting. The fern by the window was alive, technically, but only in that stubborn, not quite thriving way.

Fable, her Ragdoll cat, lay draped over the couch arm in the exact position she'd left her nine hours ago. It was possible she hadn't moved. It was also possible she'd gotten up, circled the apartment, checked all her usual spots, and returned to this exact position out of spite. With Fable, you could never be sure.

"Don't get up," Iris told her. Fable didn't.

She made a third cup of coffee she didn't need and decided to clean out the hall closet. It felt productive. Decisive. The kind of thing a person did when they were definitely fine and not at all having a quiet crisis in the doorway of middle age. Other women went to Bali or had affairs or took up pottery. Iris Quinn organized storage spaces. It was on brand, at least.

An hour later, the hallway looked like an exhibit at a museum no one would visit: *The Life That Almost Was: A Retrospective.* There was a yoga mat, still rolled in its original plastic. A leather notebook, expensive, the kind real writers used. *Chapter One* on the first page in her best handwriting. Nothing after. A pasta maker that had never met pasta. A KitchenAid attachment, purchased during a brief period when she'd convinced herself she was the kind of person who made fresh fettuccine on Sunday afternoons. Italian flashcards held together with a rubber band, the first three cards dog-eared (*Ciao. Grazie. Scusi.*), the rest pristine. A teapot, still in the box. She'd bought it the same week as the flashcards because tea was what interesting people drank. A tote bag printed with *Carpe Diem*, price tag still attached like a badge of ironic honor.

Twenty years of good intentions, perfectly preserved by never being used.

Iris sat back on her heels.

This was who she'd become. A woman who bought things for the person she meant to be, then stored them in closets where they couldn't remind her of the promises she'd made. A museum curator of her own unlived life. Every item a small act of faith that had quietly expired while she wasn't paying attention.

Fifty years old. When, exactly, had she planned to start?

Beneath a tangle of scarves that still smelled faintly of the department store where she'd bought them, her hand closed on something solid.

A small blue journal. The lock had never worked properly. It was more suggestion than security, the kind of lock that said private without actually meaning it. Inside, her teenage handwriting looped across the page with the confidence of someone who believed the world was eagerly waiting for her to show up.

After graduation, I'm going to take the Orient Express to Istanbul. I'll wear red and drink champagne and see eight countries in one week. Maybe I'll make one of them my home.

She could almost see that girl. Hair too big, dreams even bigger. So certain that wanting something badly enough was all you needed to make it happen. So sure that adulthood was the part of life where you finally got to do all the things you'd been waiting to do.

The later pages told quite a different story. The handwriting got smaller. The dreams got more polite.

Paris—someday.

Cooking class in Florence—when I save enough.

Tango lessons—after I lose ten pounds.

The entries stopped around thirty-two. Right about the time she'd started using "realistic" as a compliment.

A postcard slipped loose from the back cover. Istanbul at

sunset. Gold light on calm water. Buildings climbing the hills as though they couldn't wait to reach the top. She'd bought it at a used bookstore in college, slipped it into the journal as a promise. A placeholder for a future self who would surely, eventually, get around to making it happen.

On the back, in her own handwriting: *Book that ticket.*

Iris stared at the postcard for a long time.

Then at the ceiling. Then at Fable, who watched from the couch, unimpressed. She had never once deferred a nap or a sunbeam. Never wondered if she deserved good things. She just took them.

"I'm just going to look," Iris said, already reaching for her laptop.

The website loaded like a dare.

Venice Simplon-Orient Express. The photos looked professionally wistful, the kind of wistfulness that took a team of visual artists to achieve. Walnut paneling. Velvet banquettes. Champagne flutes catching the light. Rooms she'd only ever seen through screens, through windows, and within the pages of other people's books.

She scrolled through the images the way other people scrolled through dating profiles. With longing, skepticism, and the quiet certainty that this wasn't meant for someone like her. These were rooms for women who wore silk. Women who never...or at least rarely...spilled things on themselves. Women who knew what to do with a cheese course. Women who had never, not once, bought a cardigan just because it was both on sale *and* machine washable.

She looked at the price.

"Ridiculous," she murmured. "Completely ridiculous."

She didn't close the tab.

The phone rang. It was Robin, of course. She had a sixth sense for moments of potential self-sabotage, which she'd either interrupt or encourage depending on factors Iris had never been able to predict.

"Happy birthday. How was the cake?"

"Half chocolate, half vanilla. A question mark candle."

A familiar clatter rang out in the background. Pots, maybe, or tools. Robin was always doing something. Even her phone calls arrived with the sound of work in progress.

“So. How are we celebrating? Wine and a documentary? Finally starting that puzzle?"

"I'm cleaning out the hall closet."

A pause. That particular quality of silence that meant Robin was deciding whether to be gentle or direct. "Oh, Iris."

"I found the journal. The Orient Express one."

More silence. The clattering stopped.

"And?" Robin said.

"I looked it up."

"Looked it up how? Like, looked at pictures, or—"

"Looked at prices."

"Ah."

A pause. "And?"

Iris told her.

"I'm sorry," Robin said. "I think I have dirt in my ears. It sounded like you said—"

Robin went quiet. Iris could picture her standing in the greenhouse with her reading glasses pushed up on her head, surrounded by seedlings and the smell of damp soil. Robin's greenhouse was the opposite of Iris's closet. It was a place where things actually became what they were meant to become.

"Well," Robin said finally. "That's a lot of money for a train ride."

“A week. Through the Alps."

"Still a lot of money."

"I know. It's crazy. I don't know why I'm even—"

"I didn't say crazy."

Iris blinked. "You didn't?"

"I said it's a lot of money. That's different." Something scraped against something else. "What does it include? Meals?"

"All of them. And champagne. And a suite."

"A suite. On a train?"

"Apparently."

"With a bed?"

"And a bathroom. Marble, supposedly."

"Marble... Well. At least if you faint from the price, you'll hit something expensive."

"That's comforting."

"I'm a comforting person." There were more sounds. Water running now.

"When does it leave?"

"Three weeks. If I—I mean, if someone were to book it. Which I'm not. I'm just looking."

"Mmm."

"I'm just looking, Robin."

"I didn't say anything."

"You said 'mmm.' That's your something voice."

"That's not the point." Robin laughed. The water stopped.

"Okay. Cards on the table. Is this a real thing you're considering, or is this a 'talk me out of it' conversation?"

Iris opened her mouth. Closed it. This was the problem with Robin. She asked the questions you were trying not to ask yourself.

"Because if you want me to talk you out of it," Robin continued, "I can do that. I can list every sensible reason why a reasonable woman with a Boston-area mortgage and a public service salary shouldn't spend her savings on a European train ride."

"But?"

"But you didn't ask for the speech." Robin paused. "You called to tell me you found the journal. On your birthday. The one with all your dreams written in it."

More silence. But it wasn't heavy this time. It was just Robin, thinking. Iris had sat through a hundred of these silences over the years, waiting for Robin to finish a thought she'd never rush. It was one of the things she loved about her. That willingness to let a moment breathe.

"You know what I'd miss most about you if you got hit by a bus tomorrow?" Robin said.

"That's morbid."

"I'm sixty-three. I'm allowed to be morbid... I'd miss that you still have the journal. That you've been carrying around that same dream since before I met you, and you never let it go. Even when you probably should have."

Iris felt her throat tighten.

"Most people stop dreaming by fifty," Robin said. "They settle in. Get comfortable with the idea that this is it. You never did. Drove me crazy sometimes, honestly. All that wanting."

"Robin—"

"I'm not telling you to do it. That's your call. But I'm not going to be the one who talks you out of it either." The greenhouse sounds resumed. A door opening, something being set down. "Call me tomorrow. Let me know what you decide."

"Okay."

"And Iris? Whatever happens—happy birthday. You made it to fifty. That's not nothing."

After they hung up, Iris sat staring at the booking form.

Name. Credit card. Confirm.

I'll just fill it in, she told herself. *Just to see what it looks like.*

Her fingers found the keyboard.

Iris Quinn. The letters looked strange on the screen. Too ordinary for a train like this. She half-expected the form to reject her —*Sorry, we were looking for someone more...appropriate.*

The savings debit card was in her wallet. She'd have to get up to get it. That was a sign, probably. The universe giving her an out.

She got up. Got the wallet. Sat back down.

She typed the number slowly. Double-checked each digit. Then triple-checked, because that was who she was. A woman who triple-checked things, who read the fine print, who had never in her life made a decision this impractical.

Expiration date. Security code.

The cursor blinked in the final field. *Confirm.*

Forty-eight thousand dollars. Nearly her entire emergency fund. Every skipped vacation and secondhand coat and *I'll just cook at home* she'd been telling herself since her twenties. Decades of small denials, all sitting in a savings account, waiting for an emergency that had yet to come.

Maybe this was the emergency. Maybe the emergency was turning fifty and realizing she'd spent her whole life preparing for disasters instead of living.

Or maybe she was just tired, and lonely, and about to make a terrible mistake.

Click.

The screen flickered. For a long moment, nothing happened. Long enough for her to think that maybe it didn't go through. That the card was declined. That she might be spared from her own impulse.

Then:

Welcome aboard the Venice Simplon-Orient Express, Ms. Quinn. Grand Suite, Car L. Departure: London to Istanbul. Your journey begins.

Your journey begins. That was what the website said. As if beginning were the easy part. She sat very still.

"I just spent forty-eight thousand dollars," she told Fable. "On a train ticket."

Fable yawned. It was as close to approval as Iris was likely to get. Iris stood and walked to the window. Below, the street glistened with the last of the rain. A man with a red umbrella crossed at the corner, folding it closed as he walked. The world looked newly washed.

She turned toward the bedroom, switching off the lamp as she went, then stopped.

On the bookshelf, wedged between Austen and a guide to indoor ferns— that clearly had never been consulted—sat her old paperback of *Murder on the Orient Express.* Dog-eared and yellowed, its spine cracked from a dozen readings. She'd first read it at seventeen, curled up in a window seat, convinced her life would be full of mysterious strangers and elegant train cars and so many glamorous adventures they would eventually all blur together.

She straightened the spine with one finger. Some books you didn't outgrow. You just kept waiting for your life to catch up.

Three weeks.

2

The Orient Express was smaller than Iris had imagined. Narrower. More precise.

She'd expected something cinematic. Exaggerated, maybe, the way beautiful things sometimes were in the movies. This wasn't that. This was real.

Iris stood on Platform 2 at Victoria Station, ticket in hand, watching the cream-and-blue carriages gleam under the station lights. Brass fittings. Windows so clean they looked newly installed.

Thirty-three years of imagining, and here it was. Real. Waiting.

Now she actually had to get on it.

The platform smelled like diesel and expensive perfume and something else she couldn't quite name. All around her, porters moved with the smooth, practiced rhythm of people who had done this a thousand times.

Iris tried not to stare.

She failed.

A woman in pearls was lecturing a porter about luggage

placement, with the calm authority of someone who had never been told no. She looked to be in her fifties, posture straight out of a finishing school textbook.

Historical fiction villain, Iris thought. *The dowager who controls the inheritance.*

All those years behind a reference desk had trained her to catalog people quickly. Everyone fit into a genre. Though she had yet to fully figure out her own. Reference section, maybe—useful, organized, not the part anyone came for.

The man wearing the Bluetooth earpiece arguing with invisible markets, wedding ring catching the light—coffee stain on his shirt he hadn't noticed? *Contemporary drama. The kind where the protagonist loses everything by chapter three and doesn't see it coming.*

The young one with the artfully knotted scarf, sketchbook open, pretending not to watch everyone while absolutely watching everyone? *Literary fiction. Self-described observer of the human condition.*

And then there was the man helping an elderly woman through the crowd. One hand steady beneath her elbow, the other carrying her silver-handled cane as if it were made of glass. He was no fuss. No performance. Just quiet competence. When she thanked him, he simply shook his head and smiled—the sort of smile that didn't ask for anything in return.

Iris found herself watching him longer than she meant to.

People like that were rare. In libraries. On trains. In life.

She couldn't quite place his genre yet. *Upmarket fiction, maybe. The kind where good people turned out to actually matter.*

She looked away before he could catch her staring.

Her phone vibrated. A text from Robin.

Don't forget to steal the tiny soaps. And call me tonight. I want to hear everything.

Iris smiled and slipped the phone back into her pocket. Robin would want details. The real details, not a polished version.

A porter appeared at her elbow like a genie in brass buttons. "Your accommodation, madam?"

She handed over her ticket and smiled just enough.

His eyebrows performed a small but significant lift. "Ah. One of our finest suites. This way, please."

One of our finest.

Which meant: I didn't expect that from you.

He wasn't wrong.

Following the porter toward the train, Iris clutched her worn leather tote, the one Robin called her security blanket, and tried to look as though she did this sort of thing all the time. Everything important was in that bag: her journal, her book, her phone, her wallet. She'd insisted on carrying it herself rather than trust it to the porters, which probably marked her as hopelessly middle-class.

She didn't care. Some things you kept close.

You paid for this, she reminded herself. *You're allowed to be here.*

The voice in her head didn't sound entirely convinced.

But then her foot touched the polished step.

She stopped.

The porter paused, waiting.

Somewhere behind her, luggage wheels whispered over stone. Iris stood there, one hand still tight on her tote, the other hovering uselessly at her side.

Thirty-three years of imagining had brought her this far.

She took the step.

As she entered, Iris had the sudden urge to take her shoes off. The carpet was *that* nice, the kind of carpet that made you aware of your feet, your bag, and your entire existence as a potential source of wear and tear.

The porter moved ahead at a measured pace. Iris followed, careful where she put her eyes.

She was a tourist. Absolutely. But she just didn't have to look like one.

She passed an alcove where two men stood close together, speaking in low voices. They stopped as she approached. Nodded politely. Resumed the moment she'd gone by.

That's not suspicious at all, she thought. *Nothing to see here. Just two men having a completely normal conversation in an alcove.*

A woman in a silk robe emerged from a compartment ahead, champagne flute already in hand. It wasn't even noon. The woman's gaze skimmed Iris's tote bag—the worn leather, the tissues poking out—and her mouth tightened just slightly before she glided past.

Fair enough, Iris thought. *I'd judge me too.*

Every few steps, there was something else to take in. A brass plate etched with the car number. A small table with fresh flowers. A mirror caught her reflection and made her wish she'd done something different with her hair.

She could practically hear Robin's voice: *You're on the Orient Express and you're worried about your hair? Honestly, Iris?*

Robin was right. Imaginary Robin was always right.

The porter paused at a door near the end of the carriage. "Compartment 7, madam."

He opened it with a small key and stepped aside.

The compartment was absurdly, unexpectedly beautiful. And unapologetically so.

Midnight blue velvet on the seats and walls, so deep it looked like you could fall into it. Crystal fixtures catching the light, scattering tiny rainbows across the ivory ceiling. Fresh flowers spilling from a porcelain vase, white roses and dahlias with tiny white bells. A writing desk with ivory inlay that had been crafted by someone who took inlay very, very seriously.

Iris turned in a slow circle, feeling like a minor character who'd accidentally wandered into the protagonist's room.

The marble bathroom made her laugh out loud.

Actual marble. On a train.

She ran a hand along the counter, half expecting it to vanish, like a prop that hadn't been meant for close inspection. Marble was supposed to stay where you put it. Floors. Museums. Government buildings. It was not supposed to hurtle through the countryside at speed.

She caught sight of herself in the mirror: a fifty-year-old woman in sensible travel clothes, standing in a room that cost more than an average car, laughing at a bathroom like she'd lost her mind.

Maybe she had. Maybe this entire trip was proof.

Worth it, she decided.

"Will there be anything else, madam?" the porter asked from the doorway.

She was about to say no when she noticed the card tucked beneath the vase.

Welcome aboard, Mr. Hartwell. Looking forward to our Istanbul discussion.

She checked her ticket. Compartment 7. Ms. I. Quinn.

“I think there's been a mix-up.” She held up the card. “This was left for someone else.”

The porter glanced at it, then at her ticket.

A brief hesitation crossed his face—surprise, perhaps—before his expression settled into professional composure. “I do apologize, madam. I'll have it sorted immediately.”

He lifted the flower arrangement carefully and disappeared.

The door clicked shut behind him.

Silence settled. Thick, expensive, and slightly absurd.

Iris sat down on the edge of the velvet seat. Then stood up again, worried she'd wrinkle something. Then sat back down, because that was ridiculous.

It didn't feel real yet. Maybe it wouldn't until the train started moving. Maybe not even then.

It's a seat, she told herself. *Seats are for sitting. That's literally their purpose.*

She got up again, ran her fingers along the ivory inlay of the desk. Opened a drawer. Stationery, thick and embossed, the Orient Express logo pressed into the paper as if it expected to be kept rather than written on. Another drawer: a leather-bound guide to the journey, the menus, the history. Heavy. Serious.

She lifted it. Set it back. Lifted it again.

For twenty-three years she'd told library patrons that the inside mattered more than the cover. That appearances were not the point.

She stood there, fingertips lingering on the leather, absurdly reverent.

Finally, she exhaled.

There was a strange relief in being alone. Like the moment the library doors locked at night and the noise of the day settled into dust and paper. Except here, everything gleamed. And no one was going to knock on the window to ask her to help them print an emergency boarding pass.

She pulled the blue journal from her tote. It had survived three apartments, two relationships, and a self-help phase that involved vision boards and craft supplies that left glitter in the couch cushions. She flipped past the old entries to a blank page.

Day 1. On the Orient Express. Marble bathroom. Flowers meant for someone else. Beginning to suspect I've wandered into the wrong carriage.

She paused, pen hovering.

Then again, maybe that's exactly the right place to start.

Outside, the platform began to slip past. Slowly at first, so slowly she wasn't sure it was moving at all. Then faster. The faces blurring. The station roof sliding away to reveal the gray London sky.

The whistle sounded, long and certain, the kind of sound that meant something was beginning whether you were ready or not.

Thirty-three years of someday. Of later. Of after I get settled, after I save enough, after I become the kind of person who does things like this.

She was doing it. Actually doing it.

Her throat ached.

Through her window, London performed its farewell.

Victorian arches giving way to Georgian terraces with secret gardens. A woman at a kitchen window paused mid-dishwashing to watch the train pass. Children in school uniforms pointed and waved.

Iris waved back at the children. Then felt foolish. Then decided she didn't care.

Click-clack. Click-clack. Click-clack.

The track noise evened out, no longer announcing itself.

Then came the awareness of someone in the corridor outside her door.

They paused. The silence stretched a beat too long. The kind of hesitation that came with checking door numbers, or perhaps checking that no one was listening from the other side.

Iris held her breath, though she didn't know why.

The footsteps moved on.

Through the door, she could hear soft murmurs farther down the corridor. Tense. Hushed. The kind of voices that stopped when footsteps approached.

She found herself wondering if Mr. Hartwell knew his welcome gift had gone astray. If he was somewhere on this train right now, wondering where his flowers had gone.

She looked around her accidental palace, the velvet and

marble and wood panels that had probably heard a century of secrets, and felt the faintest hum of motion beneath her feet.

Fifty years old.

Finally going somewhere.

3

By four o'clock, Iris had unpacked.

This took approximately seven minutes.

She stood in front of the closet.

It was designed for someone whose life required a rotation of evening wear and day looks, concepts Iris had only ever encountered in magazines. The hangers were spaced generously, the shelves waiting for things that traveled with ceremony. Iris didn't have anything like that.

She regarded what she'd brought instead: a soft gray cashmere sweater that had seemed sophisticated in the store; trousers that sort of fit; three blouses in varying degrees of neutral.

And the red silk dress—still covered in tissue paper—at the far end, the hanger turned sideways, as if it had never quite been admitted.

She'd bought it in a fit of something. Optimism, maybe. Or delusion. The salesperson had called it *bold,* which Iris suspected was retail shorthand for *not for someone like you, but I work on commission.* She'd bought it regardless. Packed it. Left it untouched ever since.

The dress could wait. The dress would probably keep waiting.

She arranged her toiletries on the marble counter, suddenly aware of how modest they looked. Travel-sized shampoo. Drugstore moisturizer. A toothbrush, still in plastic, free from a health fair years ago. She was going on the Orient Express and had packed like she was going to a book-binding conference in Cleveland.

Iris returned to the main compartment and sat on the edge of the velvet seat.

Now what?

She had imagined this so many times. The train, the compartment, the long afternoon opening in front of her. In those rehearsals, she'd known what to do. Who to be.

She'd thought getting here would be the hard part. Deciding. Paying. Showing up.

She hadn't considered what came after—standing in the middle of it, with no script.

The train hummed beneath her. Outside, England unrolled itself in pale greens and grays. A field. A farmhouse. Sheep who didn't look up.

She picked up the itinerary. *Grateful for instructions.* Pathetic, maybe, to need instructions for a vacation, but there it was.

Afternoon tea. Three o'clock. Dining car.

It was ten past.

She stood up. Checked her reflection. Decided against changing her blouse.

She hadn't spent her savings to sit alone in a beautiful room.

THE DINING CAR WAS THE SORT OF ROOM THAT MADE YOU SIT UP straighter without meaning to.

Crystal, white linen. China so thin the light passed through it.

Silver catching every movement. Windows framing the countryside like something behind glass in the Louvre—clearly meant to be admired, not handled. Conversations hummed at the perfect volume. Animated enough to suggest interesting lives, quiet enough not to disturb the porcelain.

Iris spotted one empty table, a four-top near the windows, and claimed it before she could lose her nerve.

The waiter raised an eyebrow at her solitary occupation of four chairs but said nothing. Small mercies.

From here, she had a good view of the room.

At a two-seater by the door, an elderly woman sat alone with an impressive tower of petit fours. She ate them with quiet precision. One bite. Pause. Dab her lips with a napkin. Repeat. She seemed entirely content. No book, no companion, no phone. Just her and the petit fours, taken at her own pace. Iris respected that. A woman who knew what she wanted and was getting it, one small cake at a time.

Near the center of the car, the dowager and the mark—a couple apparently—communicated entirely through pointed looks and aggressive butter-spreading. The man crumbled his scone without eating it. The woman repositioned her teaspoon on the saucer. Once. Twice. Three times. Each placement somehow louder than the last.

The young man from the platform—Theo he'd told someone to call him—had taken a window seat. He sat with his tea untouched, watching the room with the kind of attention that pretended to be casual. One of the attendants kept glancing his way. And not warmly.

Then the dining car doors swept open, and a woman made an entrance.

Not walked in. Not arrived. Made an entrance.

She was in her thirties, maybe. Hard to tell. She had the kind of face that was expertly maintained rather than naturally youthful. Her silver-sequined dress caught the light at every turn. Heels too high for a moving train, but worn without hesitation. Hair that looked effortless in the way only money and time could manage.

She paused just inside the doorway. Stood one beat. Two. Long enough to make sure everyone had looked. They had.

"Edmund, darling!"

She descended on a man at a corner table—forties, with the kind of faded handsomeness that suggested better days and worse decisions. He rose to kiss her cheeks. "Victoria, my love."

She was the sort of woman who'd never met a room she couldn't dominate. The sort of woman, Iris suspected, who had learned exactly what her looks could get her and had been using them ever since. There was something almost admirable about it. And something a little exhausting.

Femme fatale, Iris thought. *And he was the mark who didn't know it yet.*

Iris realized she had been staring and looked down at her empty table. Four seats. One occupant. The waiter had already come by twice, glancing at her with the polite patience of someone waiting for a complete party.

Maybe she should have brought a book.

"Forgive me. Is this seat taken?"

Iris looked up.

The man was in his mid-seventies, she guessed, though he wore it well. Silver hair, kind eyes, the sort of face you'd trust with your spare keys and your houseplants. His clothes were well made, but it was the watch that told the story: not fashionable anymore, the kind that stays in a family and still keeps perfect time.

"I'd love the company," Iris said.

And she meant it. Which surprised her.

"Richard Hartwell." He sat down carefully, like someone who respected good furniture.

Hartwell. The name on the card. The flowers that weren't meant for her.

"Iris Quinn," she said, deciding not to mention it. Not yet.

"So what brings you aboard?"

"Birthday. Fiftieth. Lifelong dream."

She hadn't meant to say it that plainly. The words came out before she could dress them up in something more casual, more dismissive, more like the way she usually talked about the things she wanted.

Richard's expression shifted, something warm and genuine passing across it. "Claiming a dream. If only more people had the courage."

Iris didn't know what to do with that. Courage. As if booking a train ticket at fifty was brave instead of desperate. As if she hadn't spent the three weeks leading up to the trip wondering about refunds.

He signaled for the attendant. "Tea?"

The attendant appeared with a silver service—a proper pot, delicate cups, a wooden box lined with tiny compartments. "Earl Grey, English Breakfast, Darjeeling, chamomile..."

"Actually," Iris said, "I don't suppose you have coffee?"

She'd been trying to become a tea person for years. Tea was civilized. Tea was what well-read, well-traveled people drank. Tea was what you ordered on the Orient Express. But she'd never quite managed to love it.

She expected a look. Perhaps one of polite disapproval. She'd been bracing for them ever since she stepped onto the platform.

The attendant—Elena, according to the small name tag on her jacket—simply nodded and returned moments later with coffee.

Iris wrapped her hands around the cup, unreasonably grateful.

Richard raised an eyebrow. "American?"

"Guilty."

"What is it with Americans and coffee?"

“Short answer? We dumped all the tea in Boston Harbor and never looked back.” She took a sip. "The longer answer involves trade tariffs and the Civil War and a man named Folger. I'll spare you."

"A historian?"

"Librarian. Professional useless fact collector."

"Not useless at all." Richard leaned forward slightly. "Librarian. Now that is interesting."

Iris felt the old instinct kick back in. The urge to deflect, minimize, change the subject. *It's not that interesting. I just shelve books. I'm not a real academic.* She'd been doing it for years, that small preemptive retreat. Making sure no one could be disappointed in her by making sure no one expected anything in the first place.

"It has its moments," she said instead, and felt something loosen in her chest, just slightly. The relief of not disappearing herself before anyone had asked her to.

Before Richard could respond, someone slid into the third chair.

"Mind if I join? You two look like you're having an actual conversation, which is more than I can say for the rest of this car."

It was the man from the platform, the one who'd helped the elderly woman with her cane. Up close, he looked younger than she'd first thought. Late thirties, maybe, with the easy confidence of someone who belonged wherever he happened to be.

"My nephew," Richard said. "Danny Morrison. He's along to make sure I eat actual meals and don’t subsist only on honey and tea."

"Someone has to keep him alive," Danny said cheerfully. "Might as well be me."

"Iris is celebrating her fiftieth," Richard told him. "Lifelong dream, the Orient Express."

"The Orient Express." Danny looked genuinely impressed. "Now that's how you do fifty." He shot a look at Richard. "Better than some ideas I've heard."

He settled into his chair. "Uncle Richard wanted to buy a boat for his seventieth. I talked him out of it."

"You did not talk me out of it. I simply reconsidered."

"After I showed you the maintenance costs."

"Details."

“What tea is that you’re drinking?” Danny asked Iris as he began sifting through the tea display on the table.

“She prefers coffee,” Richard interrupted.

“American?” Danny smiled.

Iris laughed. A real one.

“I try to like tea. More so, I want to like tea. All the rituals and beautiful china. I just... don’t.”

“You just need to learn the tricks of the Brits," he added, pouring into his teacup. "Recipes. Tips of the trade, so to speak. We should make a point to do this while aboard."

He raised his teacup. Iris raised her coffee cup. They clinked in agreement.

A voice split the dining car, sharp and out of place.

"I was NOT looking at her, Margaret!”

Saucers stopped clinking.

The silent couple. Not silent anymore.

The woman, Margaret, stood over her husband, holding a teacup. Empty now. Tea slid from his hairline onto the table, soaking his phone, his scone, his unmoving hands.

"You most certainly were." Her voice had the flatness of something rehearsed. Years of rehearsal. "Just as you've been looking at every woman who walks by since we got on this train. Just as you've been looking at—" She turned, pointed at the sequined woman across the room. "That."

Victoria, Iris had heard Edmund call her Victoria, raised one perfect eyebrow but said nothing.

"Twenty-three years, Howard." Margaret's voice didn't crack. It was beyond cracking. "Twenty-three years of marriage. And this is what I get. A husband who can't keep his eyes in his head on our anniversary trip."

Twenty-three years, Iris thought. *Same as the library.* The universe did that sometimes. Repeated a number until you had to look at it.

Margaret turned and walked toward the door. She didn't storm out. She didn't need to.

"Margaret—" Howard half-rose, tea still dripping from his hair and cheeks.

She didn't turn around. The door closed behind her with the soft click of something ending.

The dining car was silent. Howard stood frozen, caught between sitting back down and going after her, unable to do either. The petit four woman took another bite of cake, as if marital collapse were simply part of the afternoon service.

Victoria kept her gaze on the table, her face perfectly composed, though the corner of her mouth tightened and released.

Theo was watching her. Not with interest. Not with amusement. With something sharper, more deliberate.

Victoria's eyes lifted to meet his. Just for a moment. An acknowledgment.

Then she looked away, and whatever had surfaced was already back under control.

"Well," Danny said quietly. "That happened."

"Poor bastard," Richard murmured.

"He was looking," Danny said. "She wasn't wrong."

"No. But there are ways to handle things. And ways not to."

Howard finally moved. He picked up a napkin, wiped his face, looked around the dining car at the people who found urgent reasons to look elsewhere. Then he walked out, in the opposite direction from where his wife had gone.

Conversations resumed, though noticeably quieter than before. Waiters appeared with fresh linens. Someone made a joke at a corner table, and the laughter was a little too loud, a little too relieved.

"Twenty-three years," Iris said. "That's a long time."

"Long time to be unhappy," Richard said. "If that's what they are."

"You think they aren't?"

"I think it's hard to know what goes on in a marriage from the outside. My wife and I—" He stopped. "We argued sometimes. In public, even. Didn't mean we weren't happy."

"But you didn't throw tea at each other in dining cars?"

"No. We saved the tea-throwing for home." He smiled. "More dignified that way."

"What brings you gentlemen aboard?" Iris asked, mostly to move past the spectacle.

"Business in Istanbul," Richard said. "Energy consulting."

"The kind where you save the planet, or the kind where you sell it off piece by piece?"

Richard paused, then smiled. "Depends on the client."

They all laughed. It was the kind of shared amusement that happens when strangers realize they might actually like each other.

Iris let the moment pass.

Edmund said something to Victoria that made her smile.

Theo watched. His attention stayed on her a moment longer than necessary. Not openly. Not enough to be rude. But just long enough.

When she looked up again, their eyes met across the room. It wasn't a look that meant anything. Not exactly. No signal. No invitation. Just a shared awareness, held for a fraction of a second too long.

Victoria looked away first.

Theo lifted his cup instead and finally drank his tea.

Iris filed it away. Librarians noticed patterns—books shelved in the wrong section, the regular who suddenly stopped coming in on Tuesdays, the patron who asked for one thing but clearly needed something else entirely.

Everyone on this train had a story—and not all of them were being told straight.

Outside, the countryside rolled past—bare hedges, softening light, last winter still clinging in the ditches.

Iris wrapped her hands around her coffee cup and felt something she hadn't felt in years.

A kind of alertness. A leaning forward. She felt *interested.* In people. In possibilities. In whatever was going to happen next.

For the first time since boarding, she felt like herself. Not the careful version she'd cultivated. The real one. The one she'd almost forgotten existed.

In the distance, barely audible over the train's rhythm, came the sound of a door slamming.

Margaret, perhaps, making her feelings known to the entire carriage.

Or someone else entirely.

4

The red dress was still in the closet. Still wrapped in tissue paper, waiting for a version of herself that felt ready.

Iris sat on the edge of her bed with her notebook open, pen hovering. Outside her window, the countryside had shifted—no longer quite English. She wasn't sure exactly when it had happened, only that the light had softened, and the villages looked like watercolors she had only seen in guidebooks.

Reasons to wear it, she wrote. *Birthday trip. Will definitely never be able to afford to do this again.*

Reasons not to: Very red. Very visible. Very much a dress for someone else. Red was not a color that let you blend in. That was the problem. That was also, possibly, the point.

She stared at the tissue-wrapped shape through the open closet door. It wasn't going to unwrap itself.

Just try it on, she told herself. *You don't have to actually wear it out of the room.*

She pulled it from the tissue paper, surprised by how little it weighed, and stepped into it.

She looked in the mirror. Took it off.

Put it on again.

It fit. Well enough that she couldn't pretend otherwise, which meant she had no excuse.

She looked at herself. Kept looking.

She was fifty, and the questions she asked herself hadn't changed since high school. Was she allowed to wear it? What would people think?

Different mirror. Different decade. Same girl.

She took a photo in the mirror. Awkward. Bad lighting. The kind of picture she would scroll past without stopping. She sent it to Robin.

Too much?

The reply came in under a minute.

WEAR THE DRESS.

Then, a second later:

Also you look amazing. Now stop asking permission and go drink champagne with interesting strangers.

Iris smiled at her phone and then set it down on the desk. Robin had always been good at saying the thing that left no room for argument.

She smoothed the front of the dress, then stopped herself and let her hands fall. She had a habit of tidying herself into something less objectionable—tugging hems, adjusting sleeves, making sure nothing called attention to itself.

Iris opened the door before she could reconsider.

And nearly collided with the elderly woman from tea.

The one with the petit fours. Iris had decided to file her under *English country house mystery*—the sort of wealthy widow who knows everything and dispenses her information selectively.

"You're the librarian," the woman said. It wasn't a question.

"I... yes." Iris stepped back, startled. "How did you—"

"I heard it mentioned. Dorothy Winslow."

She turned and began walking toward the dining car, clearly expecting Iris to follow.

Iris followed.

"A librarian would understand about proper documentation. I have a pressed flower collection."

The corridor was narrow. Mrs. Winslow walked ahead, talking over her shoulder with the confidence of someone who never had to wonder whether she was being listened to.

“Alpine specimens. My late husband and I collected them on our walks in Switzerland. Thirty-seven summers.” She paused at a window, gazing briefly at the darkening countryside. "Each one properly documented. Date, altitude, weather conditions. Herbert insisted on the data. He said it was what made it science instead of sentiment."

Thirty-seven summers. Iris tried to imagine it. The same two people, the same mountains, year after year. Building something together out of flowers and data and time.

"That sounds like quite an undertaking," Iris said.

"It was. 1987 was particularly fine. August fourteenth. Two thousand meters. Partly cloudy." She resumed walking. "Herbert died four years ago. I donated the collection to the botanical society afterward. They seemed a bit overwhelmed, to be honest. But it felt right. Giving them a proper home."

For a moment, something shifted in her voice. The echo of a room that used to have two people in it.

Iris knew that sound. Not in the same way, but she knew it. "I'm sure they're taking excellent care of them," she added.

"They'd better be. I left very detailed instructions." Mrs. Winslow glanced back. "You've got tissue paper stuck to your hem, by the way."

Iris looked down.

She did.

She bent to pull the tissue paper free, face warming, but when she straightened Mrs. Winslow had already pushed through the dining car doors.

Excellent start, Iris thought. *Very glamorous. Very Orient Express.*

The dining car had transformed since tea.

Same room, different mood. Candlelight now, instead of afternoon sun. Darker linens. More silver. The china looked serious. The silverware had multiplied. Iris counted three forks and felt mildly alarmed.

The room smelled like butter and wine and something roasting. Somewhere, a cork released with a soft pop. This was the kind of evening she'd imagined when she booked the ticket.

She spotted Richard and Danny at a table halfway down.

Richard caught her eye and gestured toward the empty chair beside him, not urgently, but with the quiet delight of someone happy to see another familiar face.

A familiar face. Hers.

It had been a long time since someone saved her a seat.

Danny was already pouring wine as she approached.

"Pressed flowers?" he asked as she slid into the chair.

Apparently, he had already met Mrs. Winslow.

"Extensively documented. Thirty-seven years' worth."

"Could be worse," Richard said. "Edmund's been toasting Victoria all evening. We've progressed from *luminous* to *incandescent*."

"He's working his way through the thesaurus," Danny said.

Across the room, Edmund was leaning toward Victoria again. His wine glass nearly empty—third, maybe fourth. Whatever he was saying, Iris couldn't hear. But she could see Victoria's response. The slight turn away. Posture careful. Contained.

They watched as Victoria disentangled herself, murmured something about powder rooms, and disappeared toward the back of the car.

The first course arrived—fish, foam, a drizzle of sauce that looked like modern art.

Iris chose a fork and hoped for the best.

"So," Danny said, "Richard tells me you're a librarian. What's that actually like these days? I imagine it's all computers now."

"Mostly it's people asking where the bathroom is," Iris said. "And printing. An astonishing amount of printing."

"That's disappointing," Danny said. "I was hoping for secret archives. Hidden rooms."

"We do have a basement nobody's catalogued since 1997."

"That counts."

"I've no idea what's down there," Iris said. "Which is what makes it mysterious."

Richard laughed—really laughed, the kind that catches you off guard—and then stopped. His hand went to his chest. Just for a second, something crossed his face. Not pain exactly. More like listening.

"The Bordeaux's good," Danny said lightly, reaching for the bottle. "Iris, you have to try it... Richard, tell her about that vineyard we visited in Burgundy. The one down the dirt road."

"Which dirt road? There were several."

"The one where we got lost for two hours and you blamed the GPS."

"The GPS was wrong."

Richard's hand fell away. The smile returned, tidy and practiced. Richard launched into a story about a wine estate that didn't appear on any map, a winemaker who insisted on explaining every step of the fermentation process, and a cellar that turned out to contain a family of fiercely territorial cats.

Iris laughed. Danny added details. Richard disputed them. Somewhere in the middle of it, without quite noticing when, she had stopped feeling like a guest.

Around them, the dining car kept moving.

Margaret and Howard entered together, which surprised Iris, given the afternoon's tea-throwing incident. They were holding hands. Howard's smile was fixed and careful. Margaret's expression dared anyone to comment. She positioned Howard at a table on the opposite side of the room, his back to Victoria's empty chair.

Victoria reappeared a moment later. She paused at the entrance, scanning the room the way someone does when they're calculating distance. Then she crossed to her seat.

Edmund leaned in to resume whatever he'd been saying.

She leaned back. He followed.

"He doesn't see it," Richard said quietly.

"See what?" Iris asked.

"That she's not playing hard to get. She's just trying to get through dinner."

Conversation shifted. Plates were cleared.

The main course arrived—beef in a sauce she couldn't place, vegetables set out with such care it seemed a shame to undo it. Iris ate slowly, aware that meals like this were not part of ordinary life.

Danny told a story about a conference in Geneva where he'd gotten trapped in a conversation with a man who wanted to explain the future of artificial intelligence for three hours.

Richard told a story about buying what he thought was a beautiful antique rug in Morocco. A dealer swore it had history. It turned out the history was an Amazon warehouse. He kept it anyway.

Edmund had moved on to his fourth glass of wine. Maybe fifth. His voice carried now—the particular loudness of a man who thinks he's being charming. Victoria had stopped responding entirely, her gaze fixed somewhere past him.

Iris knew this scene. Every Austen novel had a version of it—

the buffoon who doesn't know he's the buffoon. Except Austen's versions usually stayed harmless.

And then Edmund stood. Steadied himself on the table. The dining car quieted.

"I have written something," he announced. "For Victoria."

Victoria didn't move. That was what Iris noticed first. Not surprise. Not resignation. Just stillness. The stillness of someone who had been here before.

He cleared his throat. Swayed slightly. Steadied himself on the back of a chair.

"'Across the continent we fly, beneath the vast and starless sky—'"

Danny leaned toward Iris. "I can see stars from here," he whispered.

"'Your beauty haunts me like a ghost, of all the women, you I toast—'"

Victoria's jaw tightened.

"'So raise your glass and drink with me, to love that's meant eternally—'"

Edmund lifted his glass. The train swayed. Wine sloshed over the rim and onto his shirt.

Victoria did not raise her glass.

"'For you're the one I can't forget, my darling, my love, my—'"

"Edmund."

Victoria's voice was quiet, but it carried.

"Stop."

He blinked. "But I haven't finished—"

"Yes," she said. "You have."

Edmund sat down heavily. Someone coughed. A fork scraped against china.

Dinner slid slowly back toward normal. Dessert appeared—something with chocolate and gold leaf that seemed to be trying very hard.

Danny was studying the drinks menu. "They have something called the Orient Espresso."

"Don't," Richard said.

"I have to."

"Two, please," Iris said.

Richard looked at her. "Not you too."

"I'm afraid so. I love punny drinks."

She hadn't meant to say that out loud. It was the kind of thing she usually kept to herself—the silly preferences, the small enthusiasms. But Danny was already grinning at her, and she found she didn't want to take it back.

The drinks arrived in ridiculous little cups. She and Danny toasted with them. Richard refused to participate.

Across the room, Edmund had switched to whiskey. Victoria wasn't even pretending to notice him anymore.

Iris had lost track of time when a waiter appeared ringing a small silver bell.

"Ladies and gentlemen. The traditional Orient Express midnight champagne toast."

The room shifted. Chairs turned. People straightened.

More waiters emerged with trays of flutes, the glasses catching candlelight. Somewhere, someone dimmed the lamps. The whole car seemed to hold itself differently—like it remembered what it was supposed to be.

Iris watched the glasses fill and thought of Gatsby. Not the tragedy of it. The other part. The part where Nick stands at the edge of a party and thinks: *I was within and without, simultaneously enchanted and repelled by the inexhaustible variety of life.* She had always understood that line. The feeling of being inside something beautiful and still watching yourself be there.

She was watching herself now. Probably always would be. But tonight, someone had saved her a seat.

"I'll get ours," Danny said, and crossed to the nearest tray.

Iris watched him go and thought about how easy this had been. The dinner. The company. The way they'd asked questions and actually listened to the answers.

The room had gone quiet. Not silent—there was still the hum of the train, the soft clink of glasses being distributed—but the chatter had faded. People were watching the waiters move through the car. Waiting.

Danny returned with two flutes and handed one to Iris. Richard already had his.

Across the room, she saw Edmund take two glasses from a tray. He turned toward Victoria's table, unsteady, determined.

Danny followed her gaze but said nothing.

The head waiter raised his glass. The car stilled.

"To the journey," he announced. "And to those who share it."

Glasses rose. Iris drank. The champagne was cold and sharp and tasted like a memory she hadn't made yet.

Around her, people set their glasses down—on tables, on trays. A waiter moved through, collecting empties. Another followed with a cloth, wiping rings from the wood. In the soft commotion, glasses clustered together, empty and half-full, stems crossing.

The toast had barely settled when Edmund reached for Victoria's arm.

"Stand with me," he said. "Please. I just want—"

"Let go."

Her voice was calm. It carried.

Whatever he said next, Iris couldn't hear. She saw Victoria's expression change. Surprise first—then something more raw.

Then she slapped him. The sound cut through the dining car.

Edmund stumbled back.

Victoria stood very still, her hand still raised slightly, as if she hadn't quite decided what to do with it. “Don't," she said. "Ever speak to me like that again.”

She turned and walked out. Not quickly. Not slowly. But with the measured pace of someone who wouldn't be seen running away.

For a moment, no one moved. Edmund swayed.

Somewhere, a glass touched a saucer. Mrs. Winslow folded her napkin into precise thirds. Margaret leaned toward Howard and said something that made him flinch.

Edmund remained standing, as if he hadn't quite understood what had happened. Then he sat down. Heavily. Alone.

Iris looked around the dining car. The candles were still lit. The silver still gleamed. But the glamour was gone.

Slowly, people began to leave. No announcements. Just chairs pushing back, napkins set down, murmured goodnights aimed at no one in particular.

IRIS, RICHARD, AND DANNY WALKED BACK TOWARD THE SLEEPING CARS together. The corridor was narrow. No one spoke much.

After a quick goodnight at the junction, Iris slipped into her compartment and locked the door.

The red dress came off carefully and went back into the closet. It had survived. Small mercies.

She changed into her nightgown and sat at the small vanity. She picked up the handkerchief folded on the counter—linen, embroidered at the corner—and cleaned her reading glasses. Her grandmother's once. Then her mother's. Now hers.

She opened her notebook.

Midnight toast. Edmund recited poetry. Bad. Victoria shut him down. Later he said something that got himself slapped. Hard. Whatever he said, it wasn't just another clumsy pass.

Richard. His hand went to his chest and Danny jumped in like it was rehearsed. I don't think I was supposed to notice.

The red dress survived. Robin was right. I looked pretty good.

She smiled at the last line and left it.

Down the corridor, voices rose. Edmund's, slurred. Margaret's, sharp. Howard's, trying to calm things down.

So much for the romance of sleeping cars, Iris thought.

Still. She had worn the dress. Had champagne at midnight. Watched a man get slapped over something tawdry.

Seventeen-year-old Iris would have been thrilled.

Fifty-year-old Iris was too.

She pulled the pillow over her head.

Tomorrow, someone would have a headache.

Probably several someones.

5

One in the morning on the Orient Express, and Iris had abandoned the fiction that sleep was possible.

What began as whispers and soft footsteps had grown into something much louder. Much, much louder.

She sat propped against the headboard in her peacock blue robe—the one that had seemed practical in the shop and slightly absurd ever since—with her journal open, glasses sliding down her nose.

The train hummed through the dark, wheels clicking a rhythm that should have been soothing but wasn't.

Through the walls, voices rose.

"OUR ENTIRE MARRIAGE, Howard!"

Margaret's voice carried—the kind that had never lost an argument, or never admitted to. Howard's reply was muffled, defensive. A door slammed. Footsteps stormed past.

Iris polished her smudged glasses with the handkerchief tucked in her robe pocket. Monogrammed, practical, the one small elegance she'd never let go of.

Twenty minutes later, Edmund was pounding on Victoria's door.

"We need to talk! You can't just slap me and—"

"Go sleep it off," Victoria cut in, cool and final.

"Where am I supposed to go?"

"Anywhere but here. Now GO AWAY."

The pounding continued. Elsewhere, Margaret's door slammed again. Heels marched toward the dining car. Angry heels, the kind that announced themselves. They returned moments later, quicker, sharper, mid-argument about sequins and someone named Bethany from bridge club.

Bethany, had she known, would have dined out on this story for years, Iris thought, writing it down.

By one forty-five, a door somewhere was squeaking open and closed. Once. Twice.

Iris opened her door just a crack. Fresh air, she told herself, though really it was the same impulse that made people slow down for accidents.

The corridor: plush carpet that did nothing to absorb the chaos, brass gleaming too brightly, people in various states of undress and fury.

The Orient Express at night. All the glamour of a five-star hotel, all the dignity of a dive bar at closing time.

At two-thirty, Elena's careful voice floated down the corridor. "Please, sir, other passengers are trying to sleep."

Edmund was having a breakdown near the dining car, dinner jacket askew, his dignity back at Victoria Station.

"It's none of your business," Edmund snapped.

Victoria's door flew open. She emerged in burgundy silk, storming past. "Yes, Elena, mind your business. Aren't you in enough trouble already?"

Elena went silent.

Iris knew that silence. The kind you developed after years of being talked over, interrupted, dismissed. The silence of someone who'd learned that speaking up cost more than it was worth.

Just then Howard lurched around the corner. He and Victoria nearly collided in front of Iris's cracked door.

Howard's hand shot out—steadying himself, maybe, though it landed somewhere between Victoria's shoulder and her chest. The kind of accident that didn't look accidental.

"Don't touch me," Victoria snapped, jerking back.

"The train swayed!"

Maybe so, Iris thought. *And maybe men had been using that excuse since trains were invented.*

"I'm having you removed from this train."

Howard's face blotched red. "You bit—"

Richard's voice rang out from further down the corridor. *"For the love of God, would everyone please just shut up and go to bed?"*

Perfect silence.

Then Victoria laughed, sharp and bitter, and swept back to her room.

In that hush, Iris caught the faint scrape of another door shifting open, then closing again.

Quarter to three. From the corridor came the sound of dishes being collected. Danny's voice, carefully calm. "Here you are."

Elena's grateful response: "Thank you, Mr. Morrison."

Such poise, Iris thought. The staff keeping their dignity while the guests lost theirs. It was a tradition as old as service itself.

Iris closed her door, locked it. The brass lock clicked with satisfying finality.

She wrote: *Everyone awake. Everyone angry.*

The quiet continued. Her eyes grew heavy. Her pen wavered. Finally.

She shut the journal, got into bed, pulled the covers up—

Three o'clock. BANG. Something hit the corridor wall hard enough to rattle her door.

"You PROMISED!" Victoria again, fully awake and fully furious.

"I never—" Edmund, slurring worse than before.

"Get AWAY from my door!"

A slap. Crisp, decisive.

Another one? Iris thought dimly.

She sat up, fumbled for her glasses, couldn't find them, gave up. Her phone screen glowed: still no signal. Robin would have texted something perfect by now, something that would have made this funny instead of exhausting.

She pulled the pillow over her ears. It was like trying to sleep in an airport.

Half past three arrived with footsteps thundering past. *Running? On the Orient Express?*

Howard's voice, urgent and pathetic: "Margaret! Margaret, open the door! I'm sorry!"

Pounding. So much pounding.

"GO AWAY!"

"But Bethany doesn't mean—"

"BETHANY! At three in the morning you have the gall to mention BETHANY?"

More running. A door slammed so hard Iris's water glass jumped on the nightstand.

Four o'clock brought blessed quiet.

Iris's breathing slowed. Her shoulders unclenched. Her eyes closed.

Almost...

A door squeaked. Footsteps, trying to be quiet. It was the exaggerated creep of someone who thought stealth meant walking slower, not softer.

"We need to discuss the arrangement."

Arrangement, Iris thought dimly. But the word dissolved before it could take shape, swallowed by exhaustion.

She threw an arm over her eyes and gave up on the idea of waking up rested.

Half past four. Something crashed in the corridor. Glass, definitely glass.

Five o'clock. She must have dozed because she woke to more shouting. Edmund's voice, carrying from somewhere down the train. Multiple people trying to shush him.

Half past five. Footsteps again. Slow this time. Defeated. The walk of someone who'd lost an argument.

Six o'clock: quiet. Absolute quiet.

The kind that pressed against the walls, unnatural after hours of racket.

Iris lay still. Her body wanted sleep. Her mind kept replaying footsteps, slammed doors, half-heard arguments.

The hush was somehow louder than the chaos had been.

What she really wanted was coffee.

Maybe a book would help.

She remembered the glossy Orient Express brochure and its promise of a library car. A civilized touch, from an earlier vision of what the trip would be.

She pulled her robe tighter and patted her pocket by habit. Handkerchief in the right pocket. Glasses—finally found—in her left.

The corridor was suspiciously peaceful. There was no trace of the night's chaos.

The staff had worked miracles while everyone was busy screaming at each other.

As she passed one door, a faint sweetness lingered in the air. Floral, but heavy. The kind of perfume that tried too hard. She wrinkled her nose and kept walking.

A few doors down, the train swayed—or she did, hard to tell at this hour—and she stumbled, catching herself against the wall. Her palm landed in something cold and sticky.

Champagne. Of course. They'd scrubbed the carpet back to respectability but missed a spot on the brass rail.

She fished out her handkerchief and wiped her hand. Twenty-three years of cleaning up after library patrons, and here she was doing it in silk on the Orient Express. Some things transcended tax brackets.

She stuffed the handkerchief back toward her pocket and kept moving.

Iris wasn't sure where the library was, only that the brochure had tucked it somewhere between the bar and the dining car. She drifted past closed doors, polished brass glinting in lamplight, the hush broken only by the steady thrum of the rails.

At last she found it: a jewel box of a room, leather spines and a single green-shaded lamp, two armchairs angled toward each other like old friends mid-conversation.

On a stand near the window sat *Murder on the Orient Express.* Of course it did. Different edition. Same story. It felt like the universe was trying a bit too hard with the symbolism.

Iris picked it up. Who could resist? Every passenger probably thumbed through it at some point.

She'd been recommending this book since she was twenty-two. Half her life saying "If you like Christie, start with this one."

And here she was. Finally on the actual Orient Express. Holding the book in an actual library car while the train hummed through the dark.

The seventeen-year-old who'd first read it would never believe this.

She sank into one of the chairs, the leather sighing under her weight. She put her glasses on, thumbed to a random page. The murder had already happened. Poirot was gathering suspects.

Outside the window, the first gray light was beginning to soften the darkness. The train rocked gently. Her eyelids drooped.

She'd just reached the knife wounds, twelve of them, absurd, when the scream tore through the train.

High. Sharp. A rip in the morning quiet.

Iris sat frozen, the Christie still open in her hands.

6

The scream stopped.

Iris sat very still, the book open in her lap. The green lamp glowed. The leather chair creaked when she breathed. Everything looked exactly the same. Her body disagreed.

Her hands had gone cold. She noticed that first. Her fingers looked pale against the page. Breath too shallow. Ribs tight.

That had been a real scream. Not argument, not drama. Something else.

The silence came next. Not empty—wrong. The familiar rhythm of the train felt altered, thinner, as if something had been taken away.

Then the announcement came.

"ALL PASSENGERS TO THE OBSERVATION CAR. IMMEDIATELY."

There was no please. No apology for the inconvenience. Just the order, crackling through a speaker she'd never noticed before.

Iris looked down at herself. Peacock robe. Slippers.

Nothing to be done about it now.

Robin would have something to say about this. Something dry and perfect that would make Iris laugh despite herself. Iris wished she could hear it.

She got up.

The corridor was already filling with passengers.

Margaret came first. Pink nightgown, blue curlers, handbag clutched with both hands.

“This is absolutely unacceptable," she announced.

No one answered.

Howard shuffled behind her, pajama waistband slipping, eyes fixed on the carpet, trying not to take up space.

Edmund stumbled out next, his shirt buttoned wrong, hair flattened on one side and pointing skyward on the other. He saw Margaret and flinched. Saw Iris and flinched harder. Saw the uniformed staff and went pale.

"Is this about last night?" he asked no one in particular. "Because I didn't—it wasn't what it—I can explain—"

No one asked him to.

Theo appeared in his doorway. Fox pajamas. No scarf. Without it, he'd slipped genres—no longer literary fiction. *Psychological thriller*, maybe. *The kind with an unreliable narrator*. His face was blank, but not empty. Too still. Too careful.

His gaze moved down the corridor, counting heads the same way Iris was. When it reached Victoria's door, it paused. Just for a moment. Then moved on.

He didn't ask what was happening. Everyone else had—voices overlapping, questions thrown at staff who didn't answer. Theo just watched.

That was the difference.

Mrs. Winslow emerged last, a soft cloth robe belted over her nightdress, cane striking the carpet with purpose.

"Always before breakfast," she said. "Emergencies are never considerate."

Twenty-four hours ago, these had been strangers. Genres she'd assigned from a platform. Now she knew that Edmund's confidence crumbled the moment anyone pushed back. That Margaret's grip on Howard's arm was less affection than ownership. That Mrs. Winslow's cane was more performance than necessity. She only leaned on it when she wanted people to underestimate her.

Victoria was not in the corridor.

Iris waited for her door to open. It didn't.

Victoria did not strike her as someone who slept through announcements. Nor as someone who believed rules applied to her—but that would mean making an entrance late, not missing one entirely.

Staff moved past Victoria's door without knocking. Without even glancing at it.

They already know, Iris thought. And then: *Know what?*

Staff moved between them, polite and grim. "To the Observation Car, please. Quickly now."

They shuffled forward. A parade of silk and flannel and bare feet and badly tied sashes. The Orient Express, stripped of its polish. All the careful work of dressing for a journey like this—the planning, the packing, the mirror-checking—still hanging in closets.

Iris pressed herself against the wall as the others passed. Old habit. The human equivalent of shelving yourself in the back. Spine out, title hidden.

Through the windows, fog was building against the glass. Shapes moved outside. Dark uniforms.

"Howard, for God's sake," Margaret snapped. "Stop shuffling."

Danny appeared at the far end of the corridor, Mrs. Winslow on his arm. *He must have gone back to collect her,* Iris thought.

"At my age," she told him, "one takes an arm when offered."

Richard walked beside them with one hand on the doorframe.

Not leaning, exactly, but keeping contact. The way people did when they didn't entirely trust the ground beneath them. Or themselves.

Richard caught Iris's eye. Nodded. The nod said: *Whatever this is, we're in it together.*

She nodded back. Surprised by how much it steadied her.

The Observation Car had been designed for champagne and scenery and people congratulating themselves on their good taste. Now it looked like the morning after a party everyone regretted.

Pearls hung crooked. Sashes untied. More leg on display than anyone had planned for before breakfast. Iris looked for the genres she'd assigned them at the platform—the dowager, the observer, the mark. She couldn't find them now. They'd become an ensemble cast, all backstory and no plot. Waiting for the story to tell them who they were.

A steward was setting up a tea station along one wall. Cups rattling. Urn not yet steaming. As if tea could fix this. As if tea could fix anything.

Though coffee might help, she thought. *It usually did.*

Margaret claimed the settee and pulled Howard down beside her. Her fingers dug into his arm. She was hissing something at him, eyes darting to every seat.

Edmund had positioned himself near the bar with the hopeful persistence of a man who believed that if he stood there long enough, someone would take pity. The bar was not open. No one took pity. He checked his watch, checked the door, checked the bar again—as if one of these things might have changed in the last thirty seconds.

Theo stood alone by a window. Arms crossed, jaw tight, staring at nothing.

Iris found a chair near the window. Pulled her robe tighter.

She counted heads again. Margaret. Howard. Edmund. Theo. Mrs. Winslow. Richard. Danny.

Everyone except Victoria.

The door opened.

A man entered, two officers flanking him. Tall. Gray-haired. Dark overcoat buttoned to the throat. He stopped in the center of the car and let the silence gather around him.

Mid-fifties. Worn collar. No wedding ring, but a pale band where one used to be. His shoes were wrong for the weather. Good leather, city shoes. Wet at the soles.

Police procedural, Iris thought—*the slow-burn kind. Not flash. Not intuition. The kind where the detective already knew more than he was saying and would let you talk yourself into a corner while he watched.*

He stood there. Looked at them.

When he spoke, his English was precise, accented. The kind of European English that came from education, not immersion.

"Ladies and gentlemen. I am Inspector Senn. Swiss Police."

Someone coughed. A teacup rattled. The silence stretched.

"There has been a death on this train."

The words sat in the quiet. Someone made a small sound. Edmund grabbed the back of a chair.

"A passenger," Senn continued. "Ms. Victoria Halberstam. She has been found deceased in her compartment."

Deceased. The word landed oddly.

Not *dead.* Not *killed.* Chosen carefully, like something that could still be adjusted later.

Victoria.

Iris had known before the name was spoken. She'd counted the seats. Noticed the gap. Still, hearing it aloud changed the shape of things. Numbers were abstract. This wasn't. It was different when the person had laughed across the room only hours earlier.

Iris had cataloged her as femme fatale. Sequins. The practiced smile. The ease with attention.

But femme fatales survived. They didn't disappear halfway through the story. They bent things around themselves and walked away, damage trailing behind them.

Iris had read the genre wrong.

Victoria hadn't been the femme fatale.

She had been *the one who doesn't make it out.*

Edmund made a noise. His mouth opened, closed, opened. "But I—we—last night—"

He stopped. Apparently realized that bringing up last night was not his best strategy.

Theo hadn't moved. Hadn't made a sound.

Everyone else had reacted. Edmund grabbing a chair, Margaret's fingers digging into Howard's arm, even Mrs. Winslow's cane tapping the floor. But Theo just stood there. Arms crossed. Face empty.

That's not shock, Iris thought. *That's something else.*

Mrs. Winslow tapped her cane on the floor. "Well. I suppose that explains the uniforms. Though they might have let us dress first."

Senn's gaze passed over her. "This train will remain stopped until my investigation is complete. No one will leave. No one will board. Certain compartments are being searched."

Investigation. Another careful word. He still hadn't said what kind of death. What kind of investigation.

Theo's head came up. Just slightly. Something moved across his face before he smoothed it away.

What's in your compartment, Theo? Iris thought.

And then Iris had a thought—these words heard around four in the morning: *We need to discuss the arrangement.* She'd thought the voice was Theo. But exhausted, and half-asleep...how sure could she be?

"You will remain here until further notice," Senn said. "My officers will speak with each of you individually."

"How long will this take?" Margaret's voice cut through. "We have connections in Istanbul. People are expecting us."

Senn looked at her. "As long as it takes, madam. You will all be informed when we are ready for you," Senn continued. "Until then, you will remain here."

Margaret opened her mouth. Looked at Senn. Closed it again.

Edmund raised his hand. "Might we at least—I think everyone could use—"

He looked at Senn. Let his hand drop.

Senn waited.

Conversations failed to reassemble.

His gaze moved across the room. When it reached Iris, it stopped.

She felt it before she understood it. That focus. That pause.

Then she realized what she was holding.

Of course. Fifty years of putting the right book in the right hands, and the universe picks now to return the favor.

The Christie. Still in her hand. She'd carried it through the scream, the announcement, the shuffle to the observation car—hadn't even noticed the weight of it. The cover faced outward. Poirot's silhouette. The title in gold letters.

Murder on the Orient Express.

Of all the books in the library car. Of all the things to be caught holding.

Senn didn't say anything. His expression didn't change.

But she saw him see it.

She thought about turning the cover inward. Sliding the book behind her back. Dropping it casually on the seat beside her. But any movement would draw more attention, and then she'd be the woman who was trying to hide something instead of just the woman holding the wrong book.

She held still. Kept her face neutral. The way you did when a patron was looking at you and you didn't know why.

Senn's gaze moved on. He turned back to address the room, said something about cooperation, something about remaining in the car until called. Iris barely heard it.

She looked down at the Christie. Poirot on the cover, silhouette confident, mustache precise.

Outside, the fog pressed thicker against the windows. The platform had gone hazy.

And Iris Quinn—fifty years old, peacock robe, holding a novel she suddenly wished she'd left in the library car—waited to find out what happened next.

7

The book was still in her hands when the door closed behind her.

Only then did Iris notice how small the compartment was. Burgundy velvet, worn thin at the edges. Not the midnight blue of her suite. Not the public cars.

This was backstage. The Orient Express with its makeup off.

She supposed she'd expected the interrogation to happen somewhere grander. A dining car, perhaps. Chandelier light and white tablecloths, the inspector pacing between courses. That was how it worked in books.

In reality, she was in a broom closet with velvet seats, about to be questioned while wearing a bathrobe.

Agatha Christie had not prepared her for this.

She wondered if being put in the smaller room was intentional. A way of setting the tone. Shrinking her before the questions even began.

Or maybe she was reading too much into upholstery. She did that sometimes.

Last week she'd convinced herself the new carpet in the library stacks was a statement about departmental priorities. Robin had talked her down over the phone. *It's carpet, Iris. Sometimes carpet is just carpet.*

Robin wasn't here now.

And this probably wasn't solely an upholstery issue.

Senn was already seated when she arrived. He didn't stand. Didn't gesture to the seat across from him. Just watched as she hesitated in the doorway, then folded herself into the narrow space.

The door clicked shut behind her.

Their knees almost touched. She shifted back, tucking her robe tighter.

She was suddenly, painfully aware of everything wrong with the picture: bare ankles, thin fabric, hair she hadn't looked at since yesterday. No makeup. She looked like someone who'd been caught. Which she supposed she had been—just not at anything criminal. Only at being the kind of woman who hadn't packed a second robe.

There was nowhere to look except at each other.

She put her hands in her lap. Then on her knees. Then back in her lap.

Senn didn't speak. Didn't consult notes. Just sat there, perfectly still.

Iris recognized the patience. She'd seen it once before, in a reference librarian in Boston who never rushed anyone. People would sit there longer than they meant to, rearranging their questions, correcting themselves, saying more than they'd planned.

Silence had weight. It pulled things out of people.

Iris lasted thirty seconds.

"I didn't do it."

The words sounded wrong the moment they left her mouth.

Defensive. Premature. Exactly what everyone said in books, right before things went badly.

She'd read it a hundred times.

Apparently reading wasn't the same as learning.

She wanted to reach out and stuff the words back into her mouth. Couldn't. They just hung there in the burgundy room, taking up what little air was left.

Senn didn't move.

"I mean—" She tried to recover. Made it worse, probably. "I know how it looks. The book. Being awake. But I couldn't sleep. The noise. Everyone was fighting. Doors slamming. Like something out of a French farce, except nobody was having any fun."

She was talking too fast. She could hear it and couldn't stop.

Senn tilted his head. The first movement he'd made.

"The noise," he repeated, so quietly she had to lean forward to hear.

"It started around one. Maybe earlier. Margaret and Howard first. You could hear them through the walls. Then Edmund pounding on Victoria's door."

She stopped. Victoria.

The list had formed before she meant it to. Times. Voices. Order.

She drew a breath.

"That's all I know," she said.

Senn nodded once.

"What you observed," he said. Still patient. "You were awake. You heard things."

So she told him.

Margaret's fury.

Howard shuffling after her, apologizing for someone named Bethany.

Edmund's siege on Victoria's door.

She told him about Victoria snapping at Elena in the corridor. *Aren't you in enough trouble already?* And the silence that followed. The kind of silence that had a shape to it. The kind you remembered even when you didn't understand what it meant.

She told him about Howard stumbling into Victoria in the corridor. His hands landing where they shouldn't. *The train swayed.* The oldest excuse in the world. Victoria hadn't believed it and neither had Iris.

Richard's voice cutting through it all. The blessed quiet that followed. The crash of glass around four-thirty. Someone saying, 'We need to discuss the arrangement.'

"The arrangement," Senn repeated.

"I think it was Theo." She shrugged. "I couldn't swear to it."

The silence opened up again.

This time, she let it.

She was starting to understand these silences. They weren't empty. They were tests. He was watching what she did with the space. Whether she filled it. What she filled it with.

"Ms. Halberstam spoke harshly to the attendant," Senn said. "Elena. You mentioned that. What did you understand that to mean?"

"I don't know. I assumed Victoria had made a complaint."

“Are you saying Victoria looked like someone who made complaints?”

Iris hesitated.

She couldn’t tell if he was asking her to say more—or simply letting her hear how it sounded.

She thought about Victoria at dinner. The way she’d moved through the room. The way men’s heads had turned—not just Edmund’s. Everyone’s. Even Howard, mid-argument with his wife, had tracked her across the car like a compass finding north.

Iris had been that age once. Not that beautiful. Never that beautiful, but young enough to feel eyes follow her sometimes.

She remembered when it stopped. Not all at once. Just... less. A glance that didn't linger. A door held for someone else. One day you realized people were looking through you instead of at you, and you couldn't say when it had changed.

It wasn't grief, exactly. More like discovering a shop you'd loved had closed, and you couldn't remember the last time you'd gone in. You just hadn't noticed it happening until it was done.

Senn waited.

Victoria was still open for business.

Iris looked back at him.

"She seemed particular... about how things were done."

"You seem to have noticed a great deal." A pause. "For someone who couldn't sleep."

She couldn't tell if it was an observation or an accusation.

"I'm a librarian," she said. "We're professional noticers. It's what we do—figure out what people need, even when they don't know how to ask for it. Especially when they don't know how to ask for it." She shrugged again. Wished she could stop shrugging.

Something shifted in Senn's face. Not quite a smile.

"I had an aunt who was a librarian," he said. "In Bern. She used to say she knew more secrets than any priest. Because people forget librarians are listening."

Ah. There it was.

The warmth, offered so she'd step closer. The small confidence, designed to invite a larger one. She'd done the same thing herself, with difficult patrons. Made them feel seen so they'd tell her what they really needed.

"They do," she said, keeping her voice neutral. "Forget, I mean."

"And you? Do you forget you're listening?"

"No," she said. "I don't forget."

Senn nodded slowly. If he was disappointed that she hadn't taken the bait, it didn't show.

"The artist. Theo. How was he with her?"

"He wasn't...with her. He watched her a bit, though not the way Edmund did."

"How, then?"

Iris thought about it. How to explain something she'd felt more than seen.

Edmund watched Victoria the way Willoughby watched Marianne in *Sense and Sensibility.* All charm and appetite, already calculating what he could take. You could see it in the angle of his body, the way he leaned in. Wanting. Consuming.

Theo was different.

"Like he was waiting for something." She paused. "I don't know what he was waiting for. Maybe it's nothing."

"The library car," Senn said. "You went there this morning. Before the announcement?"

"I couldn't sleep. I thought a book might help."

"And you chose that particular book."

The Christie. Of course. Back to the Christie.

"It was on display." She heard how thin it sounded. How ridiculous. "I've recommended it to patrons hundreds of times. It's a classic. I thought—"

What? That it would be funny? That the universe was making a joke only she would understand? That thirty-three years of waiting had finally delivered her to a real Orient Express, and picking up the book was some kind of...completion?

"I didn't expect anyone to actually be dead," she finished.

"No," Senn agreed. "One rarely does."

The silence stretched. The morning light through the window had gone flat and gray, the kind of light that made everything look tired.

Senn's hands rested loosely on his knees. No pen. No notebook. Nothing to suggest urgency.

Iris had spent enough time in municipal buildings to recognize the type. The people who made decisions rarely looked busy. It was everyone around them who rushed.

She wondered how long he could sit like this. Ten minutes? Twenty? An hour?

She had the uneasy sense that something had already changed. Not in the room, exactly, but in him. A tightening at the edges. The patience was still there, but it had sharpened, as if the waiting were no longer for her to speak but for something else to arrive.

Senn reached into his pocket and withdrew a small plastic bag. Inside it lay a square of white cloth, neatly folded.

Her stomach dropped before her mind caught up.

The handkerchief. Hers.

She knew it before she saw the monogram, before she registered the bag or the evidence tag. She recognized it by its weight, the way the linen fell. Three generations of Quinn women had carried the same square of fabric. Her grandmother first, then her mother, then Iris, handed it at eighteen with instructions that pretended to be casual—*try not to lose it.*

And she hadn't. Through everything—two apartments, three breakups, decades of packing the same small life into the same small boxes—she had kept it. Because that was what you did with things that mattered.

"This was found," Senn said, "in the corridor outside Ms. Halberstam's compartment. Early this morning."

The floor tilted. Or she did.

Outside Ms. Halberstam's compartment. Not the library car. Not somewhere innocent, somewhere explainable.

"I—" She stared at the bag. "That's mine. But I wasn't—I didn't go to her compartment. I went to the library. Only the library."

"You are certain."

Was she?

She forced herself to think properly, the way she reconstructed a patron's steps when they swore they'd returned a book that was still showing as checked out. *Walk me through it. Where did you go? What did you do?*

She'd been in the corridor. Dark, quiet. Her hand on the wall for balance. Someone had spilled champagne on the brass rail, sticky and half-dried. She'd touched it without thinking, wiped her hand on the handkerchief, then stuffed it back toward her pocket.

Toward her pocket.

She hadn't checked. She'd just assumed it had made it there.

"I must have dropped it," she said slowly. "I didn't realize. There was champagne on the wall—from the night before, I think. I wiped my hand, and I thought I put it back, but I must have..."

She trailed off, her mother's voice rising up from half a lifetime ago. *Try not to lose it.*

She would have suspected herself. She absolutely would have.

Senn set the bag out of sight, which somehow made it worse. "Thank you, Ms. Quinn. That will be all for now."

For now. Not *you're free to go.* Not *we have no further questions.* Just *for now*, like a bookmark slipped between pages. Like he was keeping his place.

She stood too quickly, banged her knee against his, muttered an apology. The compartment was too small for graceful exits, too small for anything but this. She needed to be somewhere else—anywhere else—somewhere she could fall apart without an audience.

At the door, she turned back. She wasn't sure why.

"Inspector." She waited until he looked at her. "I didn't do this."

It was the kind of thing that meant less every time you said it.

He didn't reassure her. Just that steady, unreadable gaze.

She stepped into the corridor and pulled the door shut behind her.

The air was cooler here. She pressed her palms flat against the paneled wall and made herself breathe, told her legs to hold and kept walking even when they didn't quite want to.

She passed Richard's compartment, the door closed, his voice audible through it—low, steady, managing something. Richard always seemed to be managing something.

A porter stood at the far end of the car, motionless, hands clasped behind his back. He nodded as she passed. She nodded back. Neither of them smiled. Smiling belonged to a different trip. A different train entirely.

It was an accident, she told herself.

But knowing wasn't the same as proving. She'd read enough mysteries to understand that. The innocent suspect, unable to account for her movements. The personal item found at the scene. In stories like this, no one ever stepped in to save them.

Further down the corridor, Edmund was being escorted toward her by one of the officers, already talking, hands in motion.

His eyes locked on hers as he passed—accusatory, afraid. Iris thought about what she'd told Senn. The pounding on Victoria's door. The slap, or what had sounded like one. The whisper that crossed a line.

Maybe Edmund had reason to be afraid.

She hadn't meant to implicate anyone. She'd just answered the questions. But that was the thing about telling the truth—it didn't care whose side it was on.

She pulled her robe tighter and walked back toward her compartment.

She caught her reflection in the glass: bathrobe, hair doing something she didn't want to think about. This was who she'd brought to the Orient Express. This was who was standing in the middle of a murder investigation.

Fifty years of staying out of the way. Of being helpful and invisible and easy to overlook.

Senn hadn't overlooked her.

She thought about the handkerchief, sealed now in an evidence bag.

In stories like this, this was the moment when the amateur detective squared her shoulders and thought, *I'll show them all.*

Iris looked down at her bare feet on the carpet. Her weird, crooked toe.

She didn't feel like a detective. She felt like a fifty-year-old woman who'd made a terrible mistake—either by coming here, or by not coming sooner. She still wasn't sure which.

But she knew how to follow a thread that didn't feel right.

She knew how to sit with a question until it gave up its answer. She'd been doing it for twenty-three years, in a building full of books, for people who didn't know what they were looking for until she helped them find it.

Somewhere down the car, a door closed. Not slammed—just closed, firmly. A voice murmured, then another. The low sound of movement carried through the corridor in a way it hadn't before. Procedures beginning. People being spoken to.

The image of herself from the glass lingered, inconvenient and unhelpful.

Shoulders unsquared.

That was fine.

She'd work with what she had.

Only then did she realize the book was still in her hand.

The Christie. Bent now, slightly, from being held too long. Her thumb pressed into the cover where Poirot's face should have been.

She hadn't noticed carrying it out. Hadn't noticed carrying it at all. As if it had become part of her, the way things sometimes did when you needed them more than you meant to admit.

Murder on the Orient Express.

She closed it, finally, and tucked it under her arm. Not a shield. Not a joke. Just a fact.

8

Senn had left them waiting together. Like items in a lost and found, set out to see who would be claimed.

Iris sat with tea she'd forgotten to drink, trying not to think about her handkerchief in an evidence bag. She wasn't succeeding.

Edmund's chair was empty. He'd been taken first—passed her in the corridor on his way in, already talking, already explaining. She wondered how that was going for him. Probably not well. Senn didn't seem like someone who was impressed by talking.

Around her, the room sorted itself.

Margaret had claimed the largest sofa. Iris wasn't sure how; there hadn't been a visible negotiation when they'd all filed in. But somehow Margaret had ended up exactly where she wanted to be, and the rest of the room had organized itself around her.

Howard stood at the window, his back to his wife.

Theo had found the far corner. Hands in his pockets, watching the glass like it might tell him something. When Iris glanced his way, he looked back—held it for a moment, as if deciding whether to speak. Then didn't. Just returned to the window.

Mrs. Winslow was working her way through the biscuits. Third one since Iris sat down.

She didn't know any of these people. She'd watched them at dinner, listened through walls at three in the morning, cataloged their clothes and their arguments and their tells. But she didn't have what she relied on most—context. Here, she had two days and a lot of guessing.

Richard sat near the window with a cup of tea he wasn't drinking. Danny was beside him, close enough that their shoulders almost touched. As Iris watched, Danny said something quiet —too low to hear—and Richard shook his head. Danny's hand moved to Richard's arm. Brief. Automatic. The kind of touch that came from years of habit.

Danny caught her looking. She glanced away, embarrassed. Not because she'd seen anything private. Just because she'd been caught staring. Again.

The door opened.

Edmund stood in the doorway. His face was red and blotchy, eyes wet. He scanned the room for a friendly face.

He didn’t find one.

"I didn't do it," he said.

The words hung there. Iris knew exactly how they sounded. She’d said them herself—not an hour ago—and they hadn’t sounded any better then.

Edmund collapsed into his empty chair. His knee started bouncing immediately, cups rattling on the nearby table. He reached for his wine glass, found it empty, and just held it anyway.

The silence stretched.

"Well," Margaret said. "That was quick."

"Margaret." Howard admonished, not bothering to turn from the window.

"What? It was."

Iris thought about what she'd heard through the walls. The pounding. The desperation. *You PROMISED.* And then the slap, or what sounded like one. At the time, it had just been noise keeping her awake. Now it sounded different. Now everything from that night sounded different.

Edmund had been pathetic. Desperate. Relentless. None of those words meant murderer. But none of them ruled it out.

Senn appeared in the doorway. That same quiet presence.

"Mrs. Ashford-Pemberton."

Margaret stood. Smoothed her skirt. Lifted her chin like she was preparing for a photograph.

"Of course."

She walked out like she was doing them a favor. Howard watched her go. His hand found his wedding ring again.

The door closed.

The room rearranged itself around Margaret's absence. Which was to say: it relaxed, just slightly. Iris hadn't realized how much tension Margaret generated until she wasn't generating it anymore.

"What did he ask you?" Howard was looking at Edmund but not really seeing him. "The inspector?"

"Everything." Edmund's voice came out rough, scraped. "Where I was. What I heard. What I said to her."

"And what did you say to her?"

Edmund's knee stopped bouncing. He didn't answer.

"And the slap," Theo said from his corner. Quiet, but everyone heard. "At dinner. In front of everyone."

Edmund turned. "What about it?"

"She hit you. Then you spent all night outside her door."

"I was trying to apologize—"

"For hours."

"I loved her." Edmund's voice cracked. "I just wanted to talk."

"She didn't want to talk."

"But I needed—"

"Right." Theo shrugged. "You needed."

The room went still.

Edmund's face flushed.

For a moment, Iris thought he might stand up, might cross the car. His hands were clenched on the armrests, knuckles white.

Then he deflated. Sank back into the chair. Started bouncing his knee again.

"I didn't kill her," he said. But quieter now. Like even he wasn't sure it mattered.

Mrs. Winslow reached for another biscuit. Took a bite. Chewed thoughtfully.

Iris counted. That was number five. Or six. She was losing track.

Silence settled over the car again.

Elena moved through the room with the tea service. Her hands were steady, her face composed. She refilled Mrs. Winslow's cup, straightened a spoon, adjusted a napkin. All the small tasks that made order look possible. People thanked her without really seeing her.

Margaret returned with the air of a woman who'd just set the record straight—and expected a thank-you note.

"Howard. You're next."

Howard turned from the window. He didn't look at Margaret as he passed.

The door closed behind him.

Margaret settled back onto her sofa. Surveyed the room. Found Elena.

"He asked about the accusation," she said. Not to anyone in particular. Just to the air. "The theft."

Elena's hands didn't stop moving. But something shifted in

her shoulders. A tightening, small but visible. The kind of tension you learned to hide and couldn't quite manage.

"What theft?" Mrs. Winslow leaned forward, biscuit forgotten.

"A diamond bracelet. Victoria accused our attendant of stealing it."

The room's attention swung to Elena. Iris felt it happen—the gravitational pull of having somewhere else to look. Someone else to suspect. *Not one of us. One of them.* She'd seen it before, this particular kind of gravity. The way suspicion flowed downhill, always finding the person with the least power to refuse it.

"There was no theft." Elena's voice was quiet but steady. She didn't elaborate. Didn't defend herself. Just set down the teapot and moved to the next table.

Iris watched Elena's face. That careful composure. It was the dignity of people who understood the game was rigged. The stillness you practiced because showing anger only made things worse.

But was it just composure? Or was there something underneath?

"The attendant does have access to all the compartments," Margaret said, examining her nails. "Keys to every door. In and out at all hours. No one would think twice."

"Margaret." Richard's voice, quiet but firm. "That's enough."

"I'm simply stating facts."

"You're making accusations."

"I'm making *observations.*" Margaret smiled. "There's a difference...And of course," Margaret continued, turning toward Iris, "there's the matter of the book."

The room's attention shifted again. Landed on Iris. Stayed there.

"The book?" Mrs. Winslow looked confused.

"Murder on the Orient Express. Ms. Quinn was carrying it this morning. Before anyone knew Victoria was dead." Margaret raised an eyebrow. "Rather prophetic, wouldn't you say?"

Iris felt her face warm. "It was on display. In the library car."

"Still. Quite a coincidence."

"It's a book about a train. We're on a train. The library had a copy. I picked it up."

"A book about a *murder* on a train," Margaret corrected. "And now there's been a murder on this train. One might almost think you knew something."

"One might almost think I can read a title," Iris said, surprising herself with the sharpness. "The book is eighty years old. It's a classic. I've recommended it to hundreds of people. If that makes me a suspect, you'd better arrest half the English-speaking world."

Margaret's eyes narrowed. She wasn't used to resistance, Iris realized. Wasn't used to people pushing back. Probably no one ever had.

"I'm simply asking questions."

"You're simply implying things. There's a difference."

They stared at each other. Iris's heart was pounding. She didn't do this, didn't confront people, didn't make scenes, but she couldn't seem to stop.

"Ladies." Richard, again. The peacemaker. "We're all under a great deal of stress. Let's not turn on one another."

Margaret looked away first. Made a show of adjusting her pearls, as if she'd lost interest rather than lost ground.

Iris's hands were shaking. She put them in her lap where no one could see. Decades of professional politeness, and she'd just picked a fight with a woman who remembered every slight and forgot nothing.

Well done, Iris.

The rotation continued. Howard returned, gray-faced. Theo was called next.

He came back fifteen minutes later. No expression. He went straight to his corner.

His eyes found Elena across the room. Brief. She didn't look back. But something about the way she *didn't* look back struck Iris as deliberate.

Mrs. Winslow was called next. She stood with a sigh and brushed biscuit crumbs from her lap.

"Herbert always said I talked too much," she announced to no one in particular. "I suppose we'll find out if he was right."

She shuffled out. The door closed.

Danny brought Richard a fresh cup of tea. Set it down without being asked, the way you did for someone whose habits you knew by heart. Richard looked at it, looked at Danny, and something passed between them. Gratitude, maybe. Or reassurance. The kind of silent conversation you only had after years of practice.

Richard took the tea without protest. No deflection, no joke about not needing to be fussed over. He just accepted it. Let himself be looked after.

That was the part she'd never figured out. Not the loving...the letting yourself be loved back.

Somewhere on this train, a killer was sitting with their own cup of tea, and here she was, taking inventory of her own failures.

Get it together, Iris.

Mrs. Winslow returned, looking flushed and talkative. She settled back into her seat and reached for another biscuit.

But Iris was starting to think the eating wasn't as absent-minded as it looked. Every time someone had said something interesting this morning, Mrs. Winslow's hand had paused halfway to her mouth. Every time the conversation moved on, she took another bite.

She was listening. Carefully. Behind all the chatter about Herbert, she was paying close attention.

Danny was called next. He squeezed Richard's shoulder as if to say, *I'll be right back.*

Richard watched him go. His hand drifted toward his chest, then stopped. Dropped back to his lap. He caught Iris looking and gave a small, rueful smile.

"Old habit," he said. "Heartburn."

She nodded like she believed him. He nodded like he appreciated the pretense.

That was the thing about being observed: you learned to recognize it in others. Richard knew she'd noticed something. She knew he knew. And they were both going to pretend otherwise, because that was what polite people did.

Danny returned. His face was calm, but it was the kind of calm that took effort. The smoothed-over surface of something that had recently been turbulent.

Iris did a mental count. Edmund. Margaret. Howard. Theo. Mrs. Winslow. Danny. Herself, first thing this morning.

That left Richard and Elena. Neither had been called.

Maybe Senn was saving them for later. Maybe he'd already spoken to Elena separately—she was staff, after all, different rules. But Richard? The man who'd called Victoria "that woman" like the words tasted bad?

She filed it away with everything else.

Inside, the observation car closed in around its small rituals—cups lifted, set down, lifted again. Someone's saucer rattled. Mrs. Winslow began telling a story about Herbert's opinions on table linens, and no one stopped her, perhaps because it sounded like the sort of story that belonged to a different morning. A safer one.

Someone in this room had killed Victoria.

Someone who sat quietly now, hands folded, expression polite. Someone who had stood in line for tea. Someone who had slept badly and dressed carefully and said *please* and *thank you* like everyone else.

That was the thing about real life: it didn't flag the important parts. There were no underlined passages, no notes in the margins saying *pay attention to this*. If there were clues, they were buried in ordinary moments, disguised as manners and small talk.

She found herself doing what she always did when the stacks got disorganized: sorting.

Margaret, with her accusations and her untroubled belief that being right was a permanent state rather than a temporary one.

Edmund, whose love had begun to sound like entitlement the longer it went unanswered.

Howard, who had spent twenty-three years apologizing and might, at last, have discovered that stopping was its own kind of decision.

Elena, with keys to every door and a public humiliation that had never been made right.

Theo, who watched and waited and never committed himself to a version of events that could be held against him.

Richard and Danny, who appeared to inhabit a private world —but private worlds still had borders, and borders, Iris knew, were often where trouble began.

Mrs. Winslow, who everyone underestimated—possibly because she made it so easy, possibly because they wanted to.

Any of them could have done it. All of them had reasons—or at least reasons that passed for reasons if you didn't look too closely.

One of them was a killer. Or none of them were, and the real killer was someone she hadn't cataloged at all. A face that blended. A name she hadn't learned because she hadn't thought to ask.

She didn't know. She wasn't meant to know. All she could do

was watch, and wait, and try to notice the things other people overlooked.

Professional noticers. She'd said it like a joke. It didn't feel like one anymore.

The train hummed beneath them, stopped but restless. The fog held. And they all kept sitting there, sipping cold tea, pretending this was still a vacation.

9

They were finally released around four in the afternoon.

"You may return to your compartments," Senn announced. "Dinner will be served at six. All passengers are expected to attend."

Expected. The word that meant required but sounded polite.

The observation car emptied slowly. People drifted out like books being reshelved, some obviously in the wrong place, none of them belonging together anymore.

Iris waited until most of them had left before standing. Her legs had gone stiff. Her back ached. Beautiful chairs, she was learning, were terrible for sitting in.

The corridor was quiet. Doors closing one by one. The train still stopped, the fog still thick against the windows.

She reached Cabin 7.

The door was unlocked.

She knew immediately. The angle of the handle, the way it moved when she touched it. She'd locked it that morning, checked it twice out of old apartment habit, and now it wasn't.

She pushed the door open.

Everything looked normal. The velvet seat. The polished wood. Her bag on the chair where she'd left it.

Then she saw the drawer. Not quite closed. Open maybe an inch.

Her grandmother's voice came back to her, unbidden: *A drawer left open is a job left undone.* Iris had been seven. She'd forgotten most of what her grandmother taught her—the recipes, the songs, the stories. Not that.

She opened the drawer. Her papers were there, but wrong. The tickets on top. The passport beneath. She always kept the passport on top.

She moved to the bathroom. Her toiletries lined the counter, but out of order. She arranged them by height every morning. Librarian brain. Shampoo, conditioner, moisturizer, toothpaste. Now the moisturizer was first.

Her suitcase was unlatched.

And her journal was on the desk.

She never left the journal out. She'd put it in her bag that morning with her wallet and phone. The things that mattered. Someone had taken it out. Someone had read it. At least, she couldn't think of another explanation that made sense.

She grabbed her phone. One bar of signal, flickering but there.

She typed fast: *Someone searched my cabin. Read my journal. Everything I wrote about everyone.*

Her thumb hit send before she could second-guess it.

The circle spun. Delivering. Delivered.

She sat on the edge of the bed and picked up the journal while she waited. Her handwriting. Her observations. *Margaret: historical fiction villain. Edmund: the mark who doesn't know it yet.* Not private anymore.

Her phone buzzed.

Robin: *Was it searched by the police?*

Iris: I don't know. My door was unlocked. Everything was moved. My journal was on my desk, but I know I put it in my bag.

Robin: *Have you told the inspector?*

Iris: *Not yet. I just found it.*

A pause.

Robin: *What was in the journal?*

Iris looked at the page—*Margaret: historical fiction villain. Howard: contemporary drama protagonist. Edmund: the mark. Victoria: femme fatale.*

Iris: *Everything. Everyone. I may have sorted the passengers into genres.*

Another pause. Longer this time.

Robin: *Oh Iris.*

Iris: *I know.*

Robin: *That's very you... Good news is, if someone wanted to know what you saw, they'd know now. No more surprises. They're probably relieved.*

Iris stared. She hadn't thought of it that way. She'd been thinking about humiliation, about exposure. Not about how it changed what came next.

Iris: *I have to go to dinner soon. It's required.*

Robin: *Do you need a lawyer?*

There it was. The practical question. The one that mattered.

Iris: *I don't know.*

Robin: *Don't volunteer anything. Don't try to be helpful. Just go, eat, listen.*

Robin knew her. Robin knew that Iris's first instinct was to answer questions before they were asked.

Iris: *What should I do if someone brings up the journal?*

Robin: *You haven't done anything wrong by writing things down.*

Iris: *It feels like I did.*

Robin: *Writing observations in a private journal isn't a crime. Someone reading it without permission might be.*

Was it illegal? Iris didn't actually know Swiss law. She was an American abroad, in a foreign legal system, and her handkerchief was already in an evidence bag. Paranoid felt reasonable.

Robin: *Call me after dinner. I don't care what time.*

The signal flickered and died before Iris could respond.

She sat there with her phone in one hand, journal beside her.

Robin was right. Whoever had searched her cabin was worried about what she'd written. About what she'd seen.

She opened the journal and started reading.

The timeline from the long night. Everyone fighting. Elena collecting glasses at 2:30. Victoria at 3am. *You PROMISED.* The voices at 4am she couldn't identify. Just one word clear: *arrangement.*

But there was more. Pages of it.

She'd written about dinner. The way Victoria had entered the dining car like she expected applause. The way Edmund's eyes had followed her, hungry and obvious. The way Theo's eyes had followed her too.

She'd written about Margaret dismantling Howard's opinions one by one. About Howard reaching for wine every time his wife spoke. About the pale band on Richard's finger where a different ring used to be, and the way Danny noticed her noticing.

She'd written about Elena. *Moves through rooms like she's trying not to leave footprints. What is she afraid of?*

She'd written about Mrs. Winslow. *Talks constantly about Herbert.*

All of it. Everything she'd seen. Everything she'd wondered about.

Whoever had read this knew exactly how much she'd noticed. And how much she'd gotten right. Or thought she had.

A knock on the door.

She startled, closed the journal.

"Ms. Quinn?" Elena's voice. Calm. Professional.

Iris stood and opened the door. It was Elena.

"The inspector requests all passengers attend dinner. Six o'clock. Dining car."

"All right. Thank you."

She nodded and started to turn away.

"Elena."

She turned back.

Iris didn't know what she wanted to say. *Did you search my cabin? Did you read my journal? Are you the one who's worried?*

"Were you working last night?"

A pause. Small, but Iris felt it.

"Yes, Ms. Quinn."

"All night?"

"As scheduled."

That was all she gave. She turned and walked away.

Iris watched her go, then closed the door.

She looked at the clock. Twenty minutes until dinner.

Twenty minutes to prepare herself to walk into a room full of people who might have read every observation she'd made about them.

She picked up the journal and put it in her bag. Where it should have been all along.

She studied herself in the mirror. Hair that needed brushing. Eyes that looked tired. The same sweater from this morning, wrinkled now.

She brushed her hair. Changed into a clean blouse. Black. Simple. Nothing that drew attention.

Though it was probably too late for that.

She opened the door and stepped into the corridor.

She passed Victoria's door with its yellow tape. Kept walking.

Toward the dining car. Toward dinner with people who knew what she'd written. Toward whoever had been in her cabin, reading her thoughts.

She was going to figure out which.

Or she was going to make a fool of herself trying. At this point, the distinction felt academic.

10

Dinner felt staged.

The dining car looked almost normal. Candles lit, silver gleaming, white linen ironed flat and perfect. The Orient Express was determined to keep up appearances, even if no one sitting in it could manage the same.

Margaret had dressed as if nothing had happened. Pearls, lipstick, a silk blouse in a shade of blue that likely had a name like *cerulean* or *maritime.* She sat at her usual table with Howard, cutting her beef into precise, identical pieces and leaving them where they landed.

Howard ate steadily, eyes fixed on his plate, jaw working. He didn't dare look up. Twenty-three years of marriage had taught him when to keep chewing.

Edmund sat alone near the window. He'd made an effort — clean shirt, hair combed — but he kept glancing at the door, as if the evening might still correct itself. His wineglass was empty. His plate untouched. Whatever story he was telling himself still had room for a reversal.

Theo had taken a corner table, sketchbook open, pencil

moving. He looked disengaged, but Iris noticed he never missed a shift in the room — a chair scraping, a voice tightening. He watched without appearing to. A useful skill.

Mrs. Winslow was the only one behaving as though this were an ordinary dinner. Second helping of potatoes. Praise for the beef, delivered with enthusiasm.

“Herbert always said you should eat well during a crisis,” she announced, cheerful and loud. “He ate a full English the night before his bypass. Said it helped him think.”

No one responded. Mrs. Winslow didn’t seem to mind.

Richard and Danny had invited Iris to join them again. She’d accepted, grateful not to sit alone, but the conversation came in stops and starts.

"The beef is good," Danny offered.

"It is," Iris agreed.

They were both lying.

The beef could have been cardboard. Neither of them would have known the difference.

Richard pushed his food around his plate. He looked tired. More than tired. Smaller somehow, like the last two days had compressed him.

"Uncle Richard." Danny's voice was gentle. "You should eat."

"I'm eating."

"You're rearranging."

“I’m pacing myself.”

Iris smiled. The joke was familiar — the kind that turned concern into something manageable. She recognized it the way you recognized a well-thumbed passage, one you hadn’t looked at in years but could still find without thinking.

The door opened.

Senn stood in the doorway.

Conversations stopped in stages. The tables nearest the door first, then the ripple spreading outward until even Mrs. Winslow paused mid-chew. By the time Senn reached the center of the car, the only sound was the soft clink of someone setting down a fork.

He was carrying something. A tray, covered with a white cloth.

"I apologize for the interruption."

He didn't sound sorry.

"I have an announcement."

He placed the tray on an empty table and drew back the cloth.

Inside was a champagne glass in a plastic evidence bag. Delicate stem, wide bowl, a trace of something dried along the inside. The sort of glass you'd held a hundred times without noticing.

This one mattered.

"We have confirmed the presence of a toxic substance."

He paused.

"We believe Ms. Halberstam was poisoned."

Poisoned. The word felt like it belonged in a novel, not in her life.

Edmund made a small choking sound. Margaret's hand went to her pearls. Howard stopped chewing.

Iris found herself watching everyone at once, the way she did when a patron got loud in the library and she needed to gauge whether it would escalate. Who looked surprised. Who looked scared. Who showed nothing at all.

Danny's face had gone very still. Richard had set down his fork slowly. Mrs. Winslow was blinking rapidly, her hand frozen over her potatoes.

And Theo — in the corner — closed his sketchbook. Not startled. Not rushed. As if he'd reached the end of a page and decided there was no point continuing.

"We believe the poison was administered during the champagne toast last evening," Senn continued.

The toast. The chaos. It would be easy to remember only Edmund with his two glasses, or Danny at the tray. But it hadn't been that simple. People had been moving everywhere — hands overlapping, glasses exchanged without looking. Victoria reaching for one—but which?

"I would like to reconstruct the events of that evening," Senn said. "To understand how the glasses moved. Who stood where. Who handled what."

"You want us to act it out?" Margaret's voice was sharp. "Like some sort of parlor game?"

"I want you to show me what happened."

The way he said it made clear there was no version of this that involved saying no.

Stewards appeared with trays of empty champagne flutes. Props. Iris half-expected someone to hand her a script.

"If you would all stand," Senn said, "and take the positions you occupied that evening."

Chairs scraped. Bodies shuffled. The dining car began to rearrange itself, passengers moving reluctantly to where they'd been the night before when the toast was announced and everything was still a party.

Iris started toward her table.

"Ms. Quinn."

Senn's voice stopped her.

“You are approximately the same height as Ms. Halberstam. I would like you to stand where she stood."

The room went quiet.

Stand where Victoria stood. Play the dead woman. With everyone watching.

Margaret was watching her with that particular expression people got when they were deciding whether to feel sorry for you or suspicious of you.

Edmund looked relieved it wasn't him.

"I'm not sure—"

"You are the logical choice."

Logical. The word people used when they wanted you to do

something uncomfortable and didn't want to explain why. Her supervisor had used the same word when asking her to work Christmas Eve for the fifth year running. *You're the logical choice, Iris.* Which meant: *you don't have family obligations.*

She wanted to say no. But Senn was waiting. Everyone was waiting. And underneath the discomfort, she felt a strange curiosity. The itch to understand.

"All right."

Senn indicated a spot near the center of the car.

"Ms. Halberstam was standing here. She had moved away from Mr. Ashford's table."

Iris walked to the spot. Stood there.

The room looked different from here. Everyone facing her, everyone watching. She'd spent her career in the background. At the reference desk. At the back of staff meetings. In the corner at parties.

This was not that.

This was what Victoria had lived in, every day of her life. All those gazes. Iris understood, suddenly, why Victoria had performed so relentlessly. When everyone was always watching, you had to give them something to see. Otherwise they'd look deeper. They'd see the ordinary woman underneath the sequins.

Had Victoria been afraid? Standing here, that last night, with champagne in her hand and Edmund's desperate words in her ears. Had she felt the weight of all those eyes and understood that one of them wanted her dead?

"Mr. Crane," Senn said. "Your position."

Edmund moved forward. Shoulders hunched. Not meeting anyone's eyes. He stopped a few feet from Iris.

"You were pursuing Ms. Halberstam," Senn said. "You wanted to speak with her."

"I wanted to apologize." Edmund's voice was flat. "For the poem."

"You approached her with champagne."

"I was trying to—yes."

A steward held out a tray. Edmund took two glasses, hands not quite steady.

"Show me what happened."

Edmund moved toward Iris. Stopped. "I came up to her. I said —please, just let me explain. I had the glasses. I was offering her one."

He wasn't looking at Iris. He was looking through her, at someone who wasn't there anymore.

"And then?" Senn asked.

"She told me to let go."

"And then you whispered something to her."

Edmund's face went red. "I—that was private."

"What did you say, Mr. Crane?"

"Something intimate. I was trying to remind her of—" He looked at the floor. "It doesn't matter. It was inappropriate. She told me never to speak to her that way again. And then she slapped me. And then she walked out."

He stood there holding the two glasses, arms slack, like he'd forgotten they were in his hands.

"What happened to the glasses you were holding?" Senn asked.

"I—" Edmund blinked. "I don't remember. I was still holding them, I think? Or maybe I set them down."

"Did Ms. Halberstam take a glass from your hand?"

"I don't know. Maybe? She grabbed something. I thought she was reaching for the one I was offering, but—" He trailed off.

Senn let the silence stretch.

Then: "Mr. Morrison. Your position."

Danny moved to his spot near their table. Smooth. Unhurried.

"You were collecting glasses for your party," Senn said.

"For myself, my uncle and Ms. Quinn. The stewards were overwhelmed."

"Show me."

A tray appeared. Danny reached for it—one glass, two, three. His hands moved with an efficiency that made Edmund's fumbling look even worse by comparison. No wasted motion.

Iris watched those hands. Steady. Practiced. The hands of someone used to being useful.

"There was some commotion," Senn said. "According to witnesses."

"It was crowded. People were reaching for glasses. Mr. Crane pushed past me." A glance at Edmund. "I steadied myself against the tray. Then I collected three glasses and brought them to our table."

"Which glasses?"

"I'm sorry?"

"You picked up three glasses. Which three?"

Danny paused. Just a beat. "I don't remember. They all looked the same."

Iris agreed. All champagne glasses looked the same. She'd been to enough library fundraisers to know. The kind where you nursed one glass all night because the wine was free but the conversation wasn't worth staying sober for.

And yet. That pause before the answer.

She filed it away.

"Did you set any glasses down before bringing them to your table?"

"I might have. It was chaotic."

Margaret spoke up from her seat.

"The nephew was at the tray for some time. I noticed because I was waiting for the toast to begin. He kept picking up glasses and setting them back down."

Iris looked at Danny. His face stayed pleasant. Helpful. But something shifted behind his eyes.

Senn turned back to him. "You set glasses down and picked up different ones?"

"Possibly. I don't specifically remember."

"Inspector." Richard's voice cut in. Firm. Almost sharp. "Danny was getting champagne for our table. That's all. He has no connection to that woman whatsoever."

Iris caught it. *That woman.* Richard, who spoke about everyone with such careful courtesy. Who'd remembered the name of every porter, every steward. But Victoria was just *that woman.*

"Mr. Crane," Senn said, turning back to Edmund. "You said Ms. Halberstam grabbed a glass. From where?"

"I don't know. I thought from my hand, but maybe the table? Or the tray? It happened so fast."

"Was Mr. Morrison near you?"

"Everything was near me. It was crowded."

Senn turned to the room. "Did anyone else see which glass Ms. Halberstam took?"

"I saw her grab something," Margaret said. "I wasn't watching her hands."

Mrs. Winslow raised her hand. "I believe I saw her take a glass from the table. The one near—" She gestured vaguely toward Danny. "The nice young man. His table."

"My table?" Danny said.

"Or perhaps it was from the gentleman holding two glasses. Edmund, was it? Oh dear. Perhaps I'm not as certain as I thought."

Six witnesses. Six versions. She thought of library staff meetings. Everyone leaving with a different understanding of what had been decided. Or patrons describing the book they wanted: "It had a blue cover, I think. Or green. The author's name started with M. Or maybe B."

Memory wasn't a recording. It was a story people told themselves. And stories changed every time people told them.

She'd been telling herself one too. The one where she noticed everything. The quiet woman in the corner who saw what others missed. But she hadn't seen this.

Theo spoke from his corner. "I saw her grab a glass from somewhere near Mr. Morrison. But I couldn't say if it was from his hand, or from a tray, or from a table. She was angry. She just grabbed the nearest one."

"You were watching Ms. Halberstam closely," Senn observed.

"She was in my eyeline."

Iris noticed the deflection. The shrug that was working a little too hard. People who didn't care didn't bother explaining why they didn't care.

"Now," Senn said, "from the beginning. Everyone to your original positions. We will walk through the full sequence."

The room shuffled again. Margaret returned to her table with an audible sigh. Edmund retreated to wherever he'd been lurking before he approached Victoria. Danny moved back toward the champagne tray. Mrs. Winslow looked confused about where she'd been standing but eventually settled near the window.

Iris stayed where she was. Victoria's spot. Victoria's view.

"When I say 'begin,'" Senn continued, "move as you moved that night. Ms. Quinn, you will respond as Ms. Halberstam did—to the best of our collective memory."

To the best of their collective memory, Iris thought. Meaning everyone would move slightly differently and swear they had it right.

"Begin."

The reconstruction moved forward. Stewards circulating with trays. The toast announced. Edmund approaching with his two glasses, face tight with rehearsed apology.

Iris moved through the motions. Toward Edmund when he approached, away when he leaned in. Reaching for a glass—from where? She didn't know. No one knew.

Playing Victoria's ghost.

Elena moved through the room with a tray, demonstrating her path from that night. She paused near the center—longer than necessary, Iris thought—then continued toward the windows.

As she passed Theo's corner, their eyes met. Brief.

"Thank you," Senn said. "You may return to your seats."

The room exhaled. People moved back to their tables. Edmund retreated to his corner. Margaret began complaining about the indignity. Howard said nothing, just pulled out her chair and waited for her to sit.

Iris stayed where she was for a moment.

She was thinking about hands. All of those hands. Edmund's, shaking. Danny's, steady and precise. Elena's, professional but pausing where they shouldn't. Victoria's, reaching for a glass that would kill her.

Theo had been watching Victoria. Elena had been watching Theo. Margaret had been watching everyone while pretending she wasn't.

She was thinking about what she hadn't seen.

The moment the poison went into the glass. The hand that put it there. The face that stayed calm while doing it.

Someone in this room knew. Someone had watched Victoria drink and known what would happen next. Had they felt anything? Guilt? Satisfaction? Relief?

Or had they just kept sipping their champagne and waiting?

Iris walked toward Senn before she could talk herself out of it.

"Inspector."

He turned. "Ms. Quinn."

"My cabin." She kept her voice low. "Someone's been in it.

While I was in the observation car. My things were moved. My journal was on the desk—I always keep it in my bag."

Senn's expression didn't change. "You're certain?"

"I'm certain. I thought—I assumed you'd ordered it searched. As part of the investigation."

"Your journal," he repeated.

"All my notes. Everything I'd written about the other passengers."

Every observation. Every category she'd made, tidy and convincing—and suddenly insufficient.

Senn was quiet for a moment. Then: "Ms. Quinn, I did not order your cabin searched."

The words took a moment to land.

"You didn't—"

"I questioned you. I examined the handkerchief. But I did not send anyone to search your room." He paused. "You're certain things were moved?"

"I'm certain."

"That is concerning."

Concerning. Yes. That was one word for it.

"Thank you for telling me," he said.

He turned back to the room, already moving on to the next thing.

Iris stood there.

Someone had searched her cabin. Read her journal. Gone through her things.

Not Senn. Not the police.

She looked around the dining car. The passengers had settled back into their seats, into conversation, into the familiar choreography of dinner. Forks lifted. Glasses refilled. Voices adjusted to something that sounded normal enough.

One of them had been in her room. One of them had read her notes. One of them wanted to know what she'd seen.

Which meant she'd seen something that mattered. Something worth breaking into a cabin for.

Now she just had to figure out what it was.

11

Richard's suite was twice the size of hers.

Iris tried not to calculate what that cost. She'd already done enough math on this trip to last a lifetime. The sitting room had a settee, an armchair, a writing desk by the window. Books on the side table—actual books, with cracked spines and bent pages, not the decorative kind hotels left out to suggest their guests were literate.

The books were in three languages. She recognized the French; she thought the other might be German. A biography of someone whose name meant nothing to her. A thriller in English with a bookmark three-quarters through. Reading glasses beside them, folded, one arm slightly bent like they'd been sat on and survived it.

This was a room someone actually lived in. Even here, even for just three days, Richard had unpacked himself into it. The cashmere throw over the settee arm. A fountain pen on the desk. An empty coffee cup with a brown ring at the bottom.

Fifteen years in her apartment, and half the pictures still leaned instead of hanging.

"Please, have a seat," Richard said. He was at the sideboard, pouring wine. "I hope you don't mind—I've already decided we're drinking."

"I don't mind."

"Good. Because after that performance downstairs, I'm not sure tea would be adequate."

Danny was by the window, looking out at nothing.

The train had been stopped for hours now. Outside was just fog and darkness. The Alps were out there somewhere, but you wouldn't know it. The window had become a mirror, reflecting the three of them back at themselves.

The stillness was starting to unsettle her. That first day, the motion had been the whole point. Every mile the train covered was proof she was actually doing this—actually moving through the world. But now they'd stopped, and she couldn't shake the feeling that stillness might be contagious. That if they stayed here long enough, she'd wake up back in her apartment, and the whole thing would turn out to be nothing more than a vivid dream.

Richard handed her a glass and lowered himself into the armchair. The lowering was careful. Negotiated. His hand found the armrest before his weight found the cushion.

Iris took a sip. It was wine. Probably good wine, given the setting, but she had no frame of reference. Her usual wine came with a screw top and cost less than a hardcover. Two days ago she hadn't known these people existed. Now she was in Richard's suite, drinking wine she couldn't evaluate, while a murder investigation circled closer. It was strange how quickly the unthinkable became ordinary.

"That woman," he said once he'd settled.

"Uncle Richard—"

There it was again. *That woman.* Twice now, unprompted.

"The nephew was at the tray for some time." Richard pitched

his voice high, mocking. "As if you were skulking. As if you were waiting for your moment to strike."

"She was saying what she saw."

"She was implying something. And the inspector stood there and let her do it."

Danny turned from the window. "He has to follow every thread. That's his job."

"His job is to find a murderer. Not to let passengers slander my family."

Family. Richard said it like it settled something. As if once you said that word, the rest didn't matter. Iris had met people who thought like that. They were usually wrong.

Danny crossed to the settee and sat down. Not next to Iris—at the other end, leaving space between them. He picked up his wine glass from the side table. Iris hadn't seen him pour it.

"It's fine," Danny said. "Really. Everyone in that room is a suspect. Even Iris. Her handkerchief was outside the door."

Richard waved a hand. "That's obviously nothing."

"Is it obvious? To Senn?"

"It should be. Anyone can see she's not the type."

Not the type, Iris thought. Fifty years of being sensible, invisible, easily overlooked. The best anyone could say about her was that she lacked the imagination for murder.

"The question," Richard said, "is who did do it. Because I've been going through it in my head, and none of it makes sense."

"What do you mean?" Iris asked.

"Victoria. She was a professional."

"A professional what?"

"I don't know exactly. But you could see it, couldn't you? The dress, the entrance, the way she handled Edmund. She knew what she was doing. Women like that stay one step ahead. Or they usually do."

Iris thought about Victoria at tea. The pause in the doorway before she entered. The kind of pause that wasn't accidental. The kind that said: *watch me*. The dress. The angle of her body, positioned so Edmund had to look at her profile.

"She seemed to know what she was doing," Iris said. "Every moment felt...deliberate."

"The poem," Richard said, shaking his head. "God, that poem."

"I couldn't believe he kept going," Iris said. "Even after she told him to stop."

"'Your beauty haunts me like a ghost,'" Danny quoted, perfectly deadpan.

"Don't," Richard said. "I'm trying to forget."

"At least she shut him down," Iris said. "That part was satisfying."

"Until the toast," Richard said. "When he came back for more."

Iris frowned, remembering. "He grabbed her arm. Said something—I couldn't hear what. But her face changed."

"Right before she slapped him," Danny said.

"What do you think he said?" Richard asked.

Iris shook her head. "I don't know. But it wasn't just another compliment. Whatever it was, she couldn't just brush it off like she'd been doing all night."

"Maybe he threatened her," Richard said.

"Or said something personal," Iris said. "Something true. Something she didn't want anyone else to hear."

"He was drunk enough to say anything," Danny observed.

The room was quiet for a moment.

Danny stood and went to the sideboard. "More wine? This bottle's almost done. I'll open the other one, the one you've been hoarding."

"I haven't been hoarding it."

"You told me last week it was for a special occasion."

“Today then. I think being accused of murder seems special enough."

Robin would appreciate that line.

He brought the bottle back and refilled Richard's glass first, then Iris's. Hovered for a moment, checking the level in Richard's glass.

“Sit down," Richard said. "You're making me nervous."

Danny sat, but not before topping off Richard's glass one more time.

"I've been thinking," Richard said, his tone shifting. Lighter now, deliberately so. "About what happens after all this. After Istanbul."

He was looking at a photograph on the side table.

Iris hadn't noticed it before. A woman with gray-streaked hair, caught mid-laugh, wine glass raised toward whoever held the camera. Not a beautiful photo. A true one. The kind you kept on your nightstand because it was the closest you could get to having the real thing.

Eleanor," Richard said, following her gaze. "Seven years now. Heart failure. Very sudden."

He picked up his glass, set it down again without drinking.

"We were supposed to go to Italy that fall. Had the whole trip planned. She'd been collecting guidebooks for months. Dog-earing pages. Making lists. She had a system — colored tabs for restaurants, museums, day trips." A small smile. "I used to tease her about it. All that planning for a vacation. But that was Eleanor. She wanted to know what she was walking into."

"I'm sorry," Iris said. It wasn't enough. It was never enough. But it was what you said.

"So am I." He was quiet for a moment. "She was a cardiologist.

Forty years of telling other people how to take care of their hearts. The irony wasn't lost on either of us."

Danny was watching his uncle with a kind of gentle attention. Not hovering. Just present.

"That's why the foundation," Danny said. There was warmth in his voice. Pride, even. "In Eleanor's name. Medical research for early detection. The thing that can truly make a difference."

"Danny's been helping me set it up," Richard said. "More than helping, really. I had the idea, but he's the one who made it real. Found the lawyers, vetted the board members, handled all the parts I didn't have the patience for."

"He's exaggerating," Danny said. "I made some phone calls."

Richard shook his head, but he was smiling. "What I'm saying is — it matters. Having someone who cares about it as much as you do. Who understands why it has to be done right."

Something passed Danny's face—brief, hard to name. Gratitude, maybe. Or the particular ache of being seen clearly by someone you loved.

She watched them. Uncle and nephew, building something together. It was the first uncomplicated moment she'd seen between them since the investigation began.

She wondered how long it would last.

There was a knock at the cabin door.

Danny was up before Iris registered the sound. He crossed the room in three strides and opened the door just wide enough to see who was there. His body angled to block the view inside.

"Inspector." His voice was pleasant. Neutral. "Can we help you?"

"I have a few follow-up questions. For Mr. Hartwell. And for you, Mr. Morrison."

"It's quite late. Can this wait until morning?"

"I'm afraid not."

For a moment, neither man moved. Danny in the doorway, Senn waiting on the other side.

Senn would win. Iris knew it. Danny knew it too.

Then Danny stepped back. "Of course. Come in."

Iris should have left. This wasn't her conversation. But no one asked her to go, and she didn't offer, and somehow that felt like permission.

Senn entered. His gaze swept the room, taking in the wine, the half-empty bottle, the three of them settled in like old friends instead of people who'd met three days ago.

"Mr. Morrison." Senn's attention fixed on Danny. "You're a surgeon, is that correct?"

"Yes."

"Which means you have extensive knowledge of pharmaceuticals. Toxicology."

The room went still. Iris watched Danny's face. The pleasant expression held, but something behind it had locked down.

"Basic knowledge, yes," Danny said carefully. "It's part of medical training."

"More than basic, I would think. You would know, for instance, which substances are fast-acting. Which are difficult to detect. Which could be administered in, say, a glass of champagne without altering the taste significantly."

"I suppose I would know some of that."

"You were at the champagne tray for an extended period that evening. Multiple witnesses have confirmed this."

"I was getting glasses for our table. It was crowded."

"Mrs. Ashford-Pemberton said you were at the tray for some time. That you picked up glasses, set them down, picked up different ones."

Danny's face didn't change. "I don't think I did that."

Senn made a note. Then he turned to Richard.

"Mr. Hartwell. Earlier this evening, during the reconstruction, you referred to Ms. Halberstam as 'that woman.' With considerable... feeling."

Richard shifted in his chair. "I was defending my nephew."

"You also said Mr. Morrison had 'no connection to Ms. Halberstam whatsoever.' Were you acquainted with Ms. Halberstam prior to this journey?"

"No."

"You're certain?"

"I've never met her."

"And yet you speak of her with considerable feeling. Why is that?"

Richard looked at him for a long moment. "I don't like that type of woman, Inspector. They bring chaos wherever they go. That's not a crime, but it's not endearing either."

It was the kind of answer that sounded reasonable and explained nothing. Iris had given answers like that herself, when she didn't want to say what she actually thought.

Senn made another note. "Mr. Morrison, where were you between two and four in the morning? The night Ms. Halberstam died."

"In my cabin. Asleep."

"Can anyone verify that?"

"No. I was alone."

"Your cabin is adjacent to Mr. Hartwell's, is it not?"

"Yes."

"And you regularly check on him during the night. Due to his health concerns."

Danny's jaw tightened. "Sometimes. If I hear something concerning."

"Did you check on him that night?"

"No."

"You're certain?"

"Yes."

Senn closed his notebook. He turned to leave, then paused at the door. His gaze moved from Richard to Danny and back again.

The door clicked shut.

The silence that followed went on too long.

Danny stood by the door, not moving. His back to the room.

"He thinks you did it." Richard's voice shook. "I could see it. The way he kept circling back to the tray, to your training—"

"He's being thorough," Danny answered.

"He's being accusatory."

"He's being an investigator." Danny sat down, but not in his usual relaxed way. Perched. Ready to move. "I was at the tray. Margaret saw me picking up glasses. I'm a surgeon. Those aren't accusations, they're facts. He has to follow them."

Richard shook his head. "You're too calm about this."

"One of us has to be."

Danny looked down at his hands. Turned his wine glass by the stem. Once. Twice. Then set it down and didn't pick it up again.

Iris sat very still. Watching.

Danny had medical knowledge. Danny had been at the tray. Danny had no alibi. Richard had unexplained anger toward Victoria. Richard had said things about Victoria that suggested he knew more than he was letting on.

They were devoted to each other. Whether that devotion had crossed any lines, Iris couldn't tell. But Senn had noticed it too. She'd seen it in the way he'd looked at them both.

"It's late," Richard said finally. He rubbed his eyes. "I'm tired."

It wasn't quite a dismissal. But Iris understood. Some conversations needed to happen without an audience.

"I should go," she said.

"Tomorrow." Richard looked at her. "If we're still stuck here. Come back tomorrow."

She nodded.

Danny walked her to the door. In the narrow entrance, he stood close —not crowding, just present.

"Thank you," he said quietly. "For not leaving when Senn showed up. Most people would have."

She didn't know what to say to that. You're welcome seemed wrong. Of course seemed like a lie. She settled for nodding and stepping into the corridor before she had to find actual words.

The door clicked shut behind her.

Iris stood there for a moment, not moving. The corridor was empty. Quiet. The fog still outside the windows.

INSIDE, SHE SAT ON THE EDGE OF THE BED AND REPLAYED THE EVENING.

Senn's questions had been pointed. Danny's medical knowledge. The time at the champagne tray. No alibi. All facts, but the way Senn had presented them made them sound like something more.

And Richard—Richard had been so angry. Not at Senn. At Victoria. *That woman.* He'd said it twice now, with real feeling. For someone he claimed never to have met until this trip, she seemed to have gotten under his skin.

But then there was the foundation. Eleanor's name. The pride in Richard's voice when he talked about what they were building together.

She'd noticed the pill bottles too. In Richard's bathroom, visible through the half-open door. Six, seven, maybe more. The weekly organizer with days marked out. The way his hand had touched his chest earlier, and how quickly Danny had redirected the conversation.

Richard was sick. Probably very sick.

Iris lay back on the bed.

She didn't know what she was supposed to make of any of it.

Senn clearly had questions about Danny. Richard clearly had feelings about Victoria he wasn't explaining. But neither of those things meant anything except that people were complicated and investigations asked uncomfortable questions.

Maybe it meant nothing. Maybe she was seeing patterns that weren't there. Or maybe she wasn't.

She was too tired to trust herself either way.

12

The pounding started at midnight.

Iris had been asleep, actually asleep, for the first time since boarding, when the fist hit her door. Three sharp knocks. Then a voice, clipped and official.

"All passengers into the corridor. Quickly, please."

She sat up. Heart hammering. The room was dark except for the thin line of light under the door.

More knocking. Further down the car. The same voice, the same command.

She found her robe in the dark. The peacock blue one. She was getting very tired of this robe. Three days ago it had seemed romantic, the kind of thing a woman wore while drinking champagne on a train through the Alps. Now it was just the thing she kept putting on whenever someone decided to drag her out of bed. At this rate, she'd burn it when she got home. Or frame it. She hadn't decided which.

The corridor was already filling by the time she opened her door, and cold enough that she felt it immediately in her bare feet, creeping up through her ankles.

Edmund was closest, pajamas rumpled, hair flat on one side. He looked like he'd been crying, or drinking, or both. "What's happening? What's going on?"

No one answered him. No one ever answered him. Iris was starting to think that was the story of Edmund's life. A man perpetually asking questions into rooms that had already moved on.

Margaret emerged next, pink nightgown visible beneath a hastily tied robe, curlers still in. She took one look at the uniformed officers stationed at each end of the corridor and drew herself up to her full height. Which was considerable.

"This is completely unacceptable."

Howard shuffled out behind her. He'd managed trousers but no shirt. His chest was pale and soft and covered in gray hair. He crossed his arms over it, as if that would help. It didn't. Some things couldn't be unseen. Iris added Howard's chest to the list of things she now knew about her fellow passengers that she had never wanted to know. The list was getting long.

"For God's sake, Howard," Margaret hissed. "Put something on."

"They didn't give me time—"

"You had time. You always have time. You simply don't think."

Howard's jaw tightened, but he said nothing.

Theo appeared in his doorway. The fox pajamas again. No shirt.

He was quite a different sight from Edmund. A nice one.

She caught herself a moment too late. He'd already seen her looking. The smirk came first, slow and knowing, pulling at one corner of his mouth. Then he tilted his head slightly and winked. Not the jokey kind. The kind that made you aware of exactly how long you'd been staring.

Heat crept up her neck.

Fifty years old. Standing in a corridor during a police raid.

Caught ogling a man in novelty pajamas while a murder investigation circled closer.

Richard and Danny came out together. Richard in silk pajamas, monogrammed—of course monogrammed. Richard was the kind of man whose things had his initials on them, not out of vanity but because that was simply how things were done in his world.

Danny was in a t-shirt and pajama pants, barefoot, looking like he'd been awake already. His hand was on Richard's elbow. Steadying. Guiding.

Mrs. Winslow was last.

She emerged from her cabin as if she'd been expecting visitors. As if midnight corridor summons were simply part of the Orient Express experience, like the champagne and the white-gloved service and the scenic views. Her nightgown was patterned with small purple flowers and her white hair was pinned up neatly. Iris wondered if she slept that way, or if she'd taken the time to smooth her hair before she opened the door.

With Mrs. Winslow, it was hard to say. Some women were just like that. Ready.

"Well," she said, surveying the corridor. "This is dramatic."

Senn appeared at the far end. He walked toward them slowly, hands clasped behind his back.

"Ladies and gentlemen. I apologize for the hour. We will be conducting searches of all passenger cabins."

"On what grounds?" Margaret's voice cut through whatever thin pretense of civility was still holding.

"On the grounds of an ongoing murder investigation, madam."

"You've already questioned us. You've already taken statements. Now you're going through our things in the middle of the night?"

"Yes."

The single word hung there.

Margaret opened her mouth, closed it, opened it again. For once, nothing came out. Iris felt a small, uncharitable satisfaction at that. She'd been on the receiving end of enough of Margaret's commentary. It was nice to see someone else leave her speechless.

"You will remain in the corridor until your cabin has been cleared. You will not return to your cabins until given permission. You will not interfere with the search in any way."

"And if we refuse?" Edmund asked. His voice cracked slightly on the last word.

"You will not refuse."

Officers moved down the corridor. Two to each cabin. Iris watched them disappear into Edmund's room first. Heard drawers slide open, hangers scrape against the closet rod. Efficient. Methodical. The kind of thoroughness that made you feel guilty even when you weren't.

Iris shifted her weight. Her feet were going numb against the cold floor. She looked down at her toenails — coral, which had seemed cheerful when she'd chosen it and now just seemed like too much. Like she'd been trying too hard. Which, to be fair, she had been. The whole trip was trying too hard. The pedicure, the red dress, the forty-eight-thousand-dollar ticket. At least her feet looked nice. If you were going to stand in a corridor while strangers searched your things, you might as well have nice manicured feet.

Around her, everyone else was doing the same small shuffle—Edmund rocking on his heels, Margaret adjusting her robe, Howard still trying to cover his chest with his arms. All of them waiting. All of them about to have their drawers opened, their toiletries examined, their small privacies turned inside out.

Iris thought about her own cabin. What would they see when they opened her drawers? Drugstore moisturizer, because she'd never learned which expensive creams were worth it.

Cotton underwear, practical, the kind you bought in packs of six. A journal filled with observations about people she barely knew, written in handwriting that got messier as the wine kicked in. Nothing scandalous. Just the ordinary inventory of an ordinary woman who'd saved for years to be somewhere extraordinary.

Too late to worry about it now.

The first cabin cleared was Edmund's.

The officers emerged with a small plastic bag. Inside: white powder. It caught the corridor light, almost glowing.

"That's not mine," Edmund said immediately. "I've never seen that before. Someone planted it."

Senn took the bag. Held it to the light. Turned it once. "Cocaine, Mr. Crane?"

"I said it's not mine."

"It was in your shaving kit."

"Then someone put it there." Edmund's voice was rising, climbing toward a register that made Iris want to step back. "I'm being framed. First Victoria, now this—someone is trying to destroy me."

Margaret made a sound. Not quite a laugh. The kind of sound that said everything without saying anything.

Edmund turned on her. "You think this is funny?"

"I think you're making a spectacle of yourself. As usual."

"Someone plants cocaine in my cabin and I'm making a spectacle—"

"You've been making a spectacle since we boarded. The poems. The scenes at dinner. The pounding on that poor woman's door at all hours." Margaret's voice was ice. "Perhaps if you'd behaved with an ounce of dignity, people might believe you now."

Edmund had no answer to that. He turned away.

The corridor went silent. Even the officers paused.

Theo's cabin was next. The officers emerged with another bag

—more white powder, and beneath it, a folded envelope, some loose tablets Iris didn't recognize, a small glass vial with no label.

Theo didn't flinch. Didn't protest. Didn't do any of the things Edmund had done. He just looked at Senn with flat eyes, the way you'd look at someone who'd just told you something obvious, something boring, something not worth responding to.

"Mr. Mercer."

"It's mine. Recreational use. I'm an artist." He shrugged as if illicit drugs were the most natural thing in the world.

Senn held his gaze for a moment. "This is a crime on its own."

Again, Theo shrugged.

Two cabins searched, two bags of cocaine found. Iris wasn't sure what to make of the symmetry. Edmund had sworn he'd never seen his before, was practically vibrating with the injustice of it. She hadn't believed him. Not entirely. But now, watching Theo's flat admission, she wondered.

If someone wanted to make Edmund look bad—unstable, unreliable, the kind of man whose denials meant nothing—how hard would it be? A quick hand. An unlocked door. And suddenly the man protesting loudest was the one nobody believed.

The Ashfords were next. Their cabin (or Ashford-Pemberton, as Margaret would gladly remind you) yielded nothing of obvious interest at first. Nothing visible, anyway, though Iris saw one of the officers exchange a look with another. A look that meant something would be discussed later. The glance between colleagues who'd learned not to say things out loud.

Howard stood stiffly by the window while Margaret watched with her arms crossed, jaw set, daring anyone to comment. Whatever intimacy an anniversary trip was supposed to rekindle, Iris hadn't seen a glimpse.

Then the officers emerged with a large bottle of pills.

Senn turned the label toward the light. "Sleep medication, Mrs. Ashford-Pemberton. Quite a supply."

Margaret said nothing. Her face said nothing. But her hand moved to her throat, briefly, before she caught herself.

The unflappable Margaret, flapped. *Interesting,* Iris thought.

Edmund with his cocaine. Theo with his. Margaret with her pills. Iris had half-expected the vices in first class to be more interesting. Rarer. Vintage, like the wine. But no. Just the usual ways of not coping. It was nothing you couldn't find in any suburb.

Danny's cabin was cleared quickly—nothing of note, the officers moving through with efficient disinterest. Iris filed that away. Everyone else had something. Pills, powders, secrets in bottles. But not Danny. Which meant either he was extraordinarily careful, or he had access to what he needed without keeping it in his own room.

Richard's cabin took longer.

Danny moved forward as the officers went in. The shift was subtle. He positioned himself closer to Richard, shoulders squaring, jaw set. Not aggressive. Protective. The way you'd stand next to someone you expected to need defending.

Richard noticed. His mouth tightened.

"He has medication," Danny said, before anyone had emerged. "Heart condition. It's all prescribed. I can show you the documentation if you need it."

Senn said nothing. Just waited.

"Danny." Richard's voice was flat. "Enough."

"I just want them to understand—"

"They're police. They understand medications." Richard didn't look at him.

Danny's jaw flexed, but he stepped back. Half a step. The bare minimum.

The officers emerged with a plastic bag full of pill bottles. Orange pharmacy bottles, six or seven of them, plus the weekly organizer with its compartments for morning, noon, night. The architecture of staying alive. Iris had seen organizers like that before. Her aunt had one. Her neighbor. After a certain age, you either had one or you knew someone who did.

But there was something else. A framed photograph, small, pulled from a drawer. One of the officers showed it to Senn, who glanced at it with that unreadable expression of his.

"That's not relevant." Richard's voice had changed again. Not the irritation he'd shown Danny. Something colder. The voice, Iris suspected, that had built whatever fortune paid for silk pajamas and first-class train tickets.

Senn looked at him. Held the look a moment longer than necessary.

"Of course, Mr. Hartwell." He handed the photograph back to the officer, who returned it to the cabin.

Iris hadn't seen what was in it. The angle was wrong, and the frame had caught the light. Could be anything. Eleanor from before she was sick. A child she didn't know about. A lover from long ago. People kept all sorts of things in frames, especially things they couldn't talk about.

But she'd seen Richard's face when they held it up. The first real reaction she'd caught from him all night. Whatever was in that photograph, it wasn't for sharing.

Danny's hand moved toward Richard's arm. Richard shifted, just slightly. Enough to make the gesture miss. Danny pretended he'd meant to adjust his own sleeve.

"These are all prescribed," Danny said to Senn. "You can verify with his physician if you need to. I have the contact information in my cabin."

Of course he did. Iris suspected Danny had a file somewhere with every detail of Richard's medical history, emergency contacts, and insurance information. He seemed like that kind of nephew. Thorough. Prepared. The kind of person you wanted in a crisis and found slightly exhausting the rest of the time.

Richard seemed to be finding him exhausting right now.

"I'm sure we can verify," Senn said. "They will be returned to you, Mr. Hartwell."

Richard nodded.

And still Iris's door stayed closed.

She'd been aware of it the whole time—the sounds through the wall while she stood out here watching everyone else's secrets get paraded down the corridor. Edmund's cabin cleared first. Then Theo's. Then the Ashfords'. Then Danny's, then Richard's.

There wasn't that much to find. She didn't know why it was taking so long.

Finally, the door opened.

The officers emerged with a single bottle. Small. Orange. Familiar.

Iris knew what it was before Senn even held it up. Of course she did. She'd been taking it for three years. Had packed it carefully in her toiletry bag, tucked between the aspirin and the allergy medication, as if surrounding it with other pills would somehow make it less visible. Less significant. Less like the thing it was.

"Ms. Quinn."

Blood rushed to her face. There it was. The one thing she'd managed to keep private for three years—tucked away in bathroom cabinets, refilled at pharmacies in the next town over, swallowed quietly with morning coffee while no one was looking. The kind of privacy you built carefully, one small habit at a time. Gone in five seconds.

"It's prescribed."

"Prozac."

The word came out too fast. Too defensive. "For anxiety. It's very common. Millions of people take it."

Stop talking, she thought. But her mouth kept going.

Millions of people, she'd said. As if statistics would help...

Margaret's eye roll was theatrical. The slow, deliberate performance of a woman who had always suspected there was something wrong with people like Iris. People who couldn't just handle things.

Iris held her gaze. Let her eyes drift, just briefly, to the evidence bag with Margaret's sleeping pills. Then back.

She didn't say anything. She didn't have to.

Margaret looked away first.

A small victory. But Iris would take it.

And now everyone in this corridor knew. The little orange bottle, out in the open. Her mother had handled everything by cleaning the kitchen until it gleamed. Anxiety wasn't a word they used. You were "stressed" or "tired" or "just needed to keep busy."

Iris had thought the prescription was progress. Honesty, even. Now she wasn't so sure.

Mrs. Winslow stood apart from the rest of them, hands folded over her alpine flower dressing gown. She hadn't complained once. Hadn't shifted or shuffled or asked how much longer. While the rest of them fidgeted like children, Mrs. Winslow simply waited. Watching the corridor the way she might watch a garden —patiently, as if something interesting would eventually bloom.

"It's always the same," she said to Margaret, who definitely wasn't interested. “A good arrangement must balance everything."

Arrangement.

The word caught.

Four in the morning. The corridor dark, the chaos of that night finally settling. A voice through the wall, Theo's, she'd thought. Low. Urgent. *We need to discuss the arrangement.* She'd mentioned it to Senn. What else could she do?

Iris found herself looking at Theo again.

He was already looking back. The smirk was gone. In its place, something still. Watchful. The fox pajamas suddenly seemed less whimsical.

She looked away. Found a spot on the carpet and studied it.

Around her, the corridor churned on. Edmund protesting. Margaret cutting him down. Howard murmuring apologies to no one. The noise swallowed everything, and by the time it settled, the moment had passed.

The officers emerged from Mrs. Winslow's cabin. Empty-handed. Mrs. Winslow nodded as if she'd expected nothing less. As if it would have been absurd to find anything, as if she had been above suspicion all along, simply by virtue of being herself.

To be fair, Iris couldn't imagine Mrs. Winslow hiding anything more scandalous than an extra biscuit.

The staff quarters were searched last. Iris hadn't thought about it, hadn't considered that Elena and the other attendants would be subjected to the same indignity. But of course they would. Everyone meant everyone.

She couldn't see the search, but she heard the murmur that passed through the corridor afterward. Saw the way two officers emerged from the staff car carrying evidence bags.

Something silver. Something silk.

Victoria had accused Elena of stealing a bracelet. Iris remembered it now—Margaret mentioning the accusation during the questioning, the way Elena's shoulders had tightened almost imperceptibly. *There was no theft.* That's all she'd said. No defense. No explanation. Just the quiet dignity of someone who'd learned that defending yourself only made things worse.

Elena stood very still near the dining car entrance. Her face revealed nothing. But her hands, clasped in front of her, were white at the knuckles.

One by one, they were allowed back into their cabins.

Iris closed her door. Locked it. Leaned against it.

The room looked the same as before. The velvet still velvet. The brass still gleaming. The officers had been careful, professional, but she could see the small signs of disturbance. The drawer not quite closed. Her suitcase slightly askew. Someone had moved her toothbrush. Bristles-down now, leaning against the marble. She always left it bristles-up. One of those habits she'd never examined and couldn't have explained.

She put it back. It was a small thing. But it was not a small thing.

They'd touched everything. Seen everything.

She sat on the edge of the bed. The same bed she'd been so thrilled to see three days ago, with its crisp white sheets and its ridiculous thread count. Now it was just a bed.

Through the wall, she could hear Edmund's voice. Still going. Still complaining about the cocaine, the injustice of it all. The man had stamina, she'd give him that.

She should call Robin. Robin would want to know about this—the midnight searches, the evidence bags, Margaret's sleeping pills, Iris's Prozac held up for everyone to see. Robin would have something to say about all of it.

But her phone was in her bag, and her bag was across the room, and she was so tired.

She wondered if Fable missed her. Probably not. Fable had spent the last week doing exactly what she did every week—sleeping in sunbeams, eating when hungry, existing without requiring emotional validation from anyone. It was an approach to life Iris envied.

She lay back and stared at the ceiling.

Iris turned onto her side.

She kept thinking about Richard. The photograph tucked in his drawer. The way his voice had gone cold when he'd said it wasn't relevant. The anger when he talked about Victoria—*that woman*—for someone he claimed never to have met.

It reminded her of *And Then There Were None*. Another Christie. The way the killer in that one had hidden in plain sight. Old, dying, using their own mortality as cover. Everyone so busy looking at the obvious suspects that they never considered the person who seemed above it all.

Richard was sick. Richard was angry at a dead woman. Richard had a devoted nephew with medical knowledge who would probably do anything he asked.

Or maybe she was just tired and seeing Christie plots in ordinary grief. A dying man who'd lost his wife and was watching his nephew get accused of murder. Of course he was angry. Of course he kept things private.

Through the wall, Edmund finally went quiet.

Iris closed her eyes and hoped he stayed that way.

13

The dining car was attempting normalcy the way a hostess attempts conversation after someone has said something unforgivable at dinner. Bright smile. Fresh linens. Nothing to see here.

Iris wasn't fooled. Neither, she suspected, was anyone else.

She took her usual table by the window. Ordered coffee. Watched the other passengers arrive.

This was the problem with midnight searches. You learned things you couldn't unlearn. Howard's chest hair would live in her memory forever now. Margaret's sleeping pills—that industrial-sized bottle—explained why someone so desperate to control everything around her might need help surrendering control at night.

You couldn't give that information back. It just sat there, taking up space, like books no one wanted to read but weren't old enough to weed from the collection.

Margaret arrived first. Pearls. Lipstick. Posture that could balance a book.

But something was off.

It took Iris a moment to place it. The pearls were the same. The lipstick was the same shade of fire engine red she'd worn every day. But Margaret's hair—always sculpted into precise waves—had a slight flatness on the left side. And her blouse, cream silk, was buttoned one hole off. The kind of mistake you made when your hands were shaking, or when you'd dressed in the dark, or when you simply hadn't checked the mirror the way you always checked the mirror.

Margaret moved through the dining car like the previous night had happened to someone else. But her armor had slipped. Just slightly. Just enough to notice.

She paused at Iris's table.

"I do hope you slept well," Margaret said. "After all that excitement."

The emphasis on *excitement* made it clear she meant *Prozac.* She meant the bottle Senn had held up for everyone to see.

Iris looked at Margaret's mis-buttoned blouse. Considered mentioning it. Considered saying something about sleeping pills, about needing a pharmacy to get through twenty-three years of marriage, about the way Margaret's hand had gone to her throat when Senn held up that bottle.

She didn't.

"Well enough," Iris said. "Thank you for asking."

Margaret's eyes narrowed slightly, as if she'd expected a fight and wasn't sure what to do without one. She moved on without another word.

It wasn't a victory. But Iris had learned something. Margaret was rattled. Margaret, who had sailed through the tea-throwing incident and the midnight searches and every other indignity with her head high—Margaret was coming undone.

Worth knowing.

Howard followed. He had managed a proper shirt this time. Small mercies.

Edmund arrived looking terrible. He sat alone, ordered tea he didn't touch, and kept patting his jacket pockets as if searching for something he'd already lost.

Theo sat in the far corner, sketchbook open, pencil moving. But his eyes weren't on the page. They were on Edmund.

Richard and Danny came in together.

Richard looked more than tired. Diminished, somehow, like the midnight search had taken something out of him that sleep couldn't restore. Danny pulled out his chair, waited for him to sit, then took his own seat where he could watch the room and Richard at the same time.

Danny caught her eye across the room. Nodded. She nodded back.

Elena emerged from the service area. Eyes red. Face carefully blank.

She was still working—still carrying trays, still moving efficiently through the car. But there was a brittleness to it now. The difference between someone doing their job and someone clinging to it as the only thing they had left.

Silver and silk in evidence bags. Victoria's accusations, now official.

Elena poured hot water for Margaret. Margaret said something Iris couldn't hear—her voice pitched low, deliberately so. Elena's expression didn't change, but her hand tightened on the pot handle. She said something back. Also too quiet to hear. But her chin lifted slightly as she said it.

Good for you, Iris thought.

Elena moved on to the next table, where two women Iris had seen but never spoken to were leaning toward each other with the particular intimacy of shared gossip.

"—powder room, of all places," one of them said. "As if Victoria Halberstam would use a public—"

She stopped as Elena approached with the tea service, smiled brightly, thanked her with unnecessary warmth, and didn't resume talking until Elena had moved well out of earshot.

Iris couldn't hear the rest. But she didn't need to. The shape of the conversation was clear enough. Victoria's things found in Elena's quarters. Elena's explanation—unconvincing, apparently. The verdict already reached in the court of the dining car.

Elena moved toward Senn's table.

Iris hadn't noticed him until now. He'd been there when she arrived, she realized. Positioned where he could see the whole room without being obvious about it. A cup of tea in front of him. A notebook open on the table.

He wasn't writing. Just watching.

Elena stopped at his table. Lifted the pot. He nodded. She poured.

And while she stood there, blocking part of Iris's view, Senn looked down at his notebook. Turned a page.

Elena moved away.

The notebook was still open. Angled slightly toward where Iris sat.

She shouldn't look. It was rude. It was probably illegal. It was certainly the kind of thing that would make her look guilty if anyone noticed.

She looked.

It was too far away to read properly. The handwriting small, European, slanting hard to the right. But she'd spent decades making sense of half-legible request slips and scribbled call numbers. This wasn't so different.

Names. She could make out names. A list of them, running down the left side of the page.

One had been underlined twice. The capital letter tall and angular. A *T*, she thought. Then the downstroke of an *h*. *Theo*.

One was circled. Shorter. The loop of an *E*, a cluster of letters she couldn't quite resolve, the tail of an *a*. *Elena*.

And a third, off to the side. Not underlined, not circled, but set apart. A question mark next to it.

The first letter had a long descending tail. *Q*.

Her stomach dropped.

Q for *Quinn*. *Q* for *questioned*.

Senn closed the notebook.

He looked up. Directly at her.

Caught.

Her face went hot. The way it had in the corridor last night, when they'd held up her Prozac for everyone to see. The way it always did when she was caught doing something she shouldn't—reading someone's mail, eavesdropping on conversations.

She hadn't done anything wrong—technically. She'd just been looking.

But Senn didn't look away. He didn't smile. He just studied her with those patient eyes.

She should look away first. Break the moment. Pretend she hadn't noticed.

She didn't.

Then he stood.

He walked toward her table. Slowly. The way he did everything.

"Ms. Quinn." His voice was pleasant. Mild. "A word, if you don't mind."

It wasn't a question.

She followed him out of the dining car, past the bar car where a porter was polishing glasses that were already clean, through a connecting door that rattled as the train sat motionless.

Still, the fog pressed against every window. No mountains. No sky. Just white, as if the world beyond the train had simply stopped existing.

THE SMALL COMPARTMENT AGAIN. SHE NOTICED THINGS SHE'D MISSED the first time—the velvet worn thin where countless elbows had rested, a small tear in the curtain, a water stain on the ceiling shaped like Italy. Or maybe France. Geography had never been her strength.

But something had changed. Senn sat across from her with his notebook closed. Not consulting anything. Just looking at her with an expression she couldn't read.

"Ms. Quinn," he said. "I've been conducting background inquiries. On all the passengers." A pause. "Yours was... interesting."

She waited.

"Interesting how?"

"You've worked at the same library for twenty-three years. You live alone. No children—"

"I have a cat," Iris interrupted, having no idea why she said that.

He continued. "You have a modest salary. Very modest. Libraries aren't known for generous compensation."

"They're not."

"Which is why I found it curious that three weeks ago, you withdrew forty-eight thousand dollars from your savings account." He let that number sit between them. "And then you boarded this train. The most expensive journey in Europe."

"The ticket cost what it cost."

"Yes. Almost exactly what you had." His head tilted. "That's quite a coincidence."

"It's not a coincidence. It's arithmetic."

His mouth moved. Not quite a smile.

"Ms. Quinn, do you know what Victoria Halberstam did for a living?"

The shift caught her off guard.

"No."

Senn leaned back. "Victoria Halberstam was a professional. She targeted wealthy older men. Charmed them. Extracted significant sums. Various names, various cities. At least a decade of this, possibly longer."

A con artist. Of course. *Femme fatale*, Iris had written in her journal. She'd meant it as a type. Turned out it was a profession.

"I didn't know that."

"No?" Senn's voice stayed mild. "Your journal suggests you notice quite a lot. Very detailed observations. Almost as if you were taking notes for someone."

"For myself."

"For yourself." He repeated it without inflection. "Con artists often work in pairs, Ms. Quinn. One to charm. One to gather information. One to be seen..." He paused. "And one to remain invisible."

The implication landed like a slap.

"You think I was working with her."

"I think it's a possibility I have to consider." He spread his hands, a gesture of reasonableness that felt anything but. "A woman empties her savings. Boards a train full of wealthy passengers. A con artist is murdered. The woman's handkerchief is found outside the victim's door. The woman keeps detailed notes on everyone she meets." He paused. "What would you conclude?"

Iris stared at him.

So in Senn's version, Victoria was the honey trap and Iris was —what? The secretary. She could be charming. She could be a honey trap if she wanted. Probably.

"The handkerchief," she said. "I wiped champagne off my hand. Six in the morning. On my way to the library car."

"So you've said."

"Because that's what happened."

Senn waited.

"I write things down because—" She stopped. Because why? Because it made her feel like she was participating in her own life instead of just watching it? Because the journal was the only place she'd ever been honest about what she saw?

"Because I've always been better at observing than participating," she said. "It's not a skill. It's a limitation."

Something shifted in Senn's expression. She couldn't tell if it was belief or just interest.

"And the savings?"

"I turned fifty." She heard how that sounded. Not like an explanation. Like an excuse. "I had a closet full of things I'd bought for someone I never became. Italian flashcards I never used. A pasta maker still in the box. Twenty-six years of saving for someday, and someday never came." She looked at her hands. "So I spent it. All of it. On something I'd wanted since I was seventeen."

Most people don't liquidate their savings for a train ticket," Senn said.

"Most people probably have something better to spend it on."

The compartment was quiet.

"I'm not a criminal," Iris said. "I'm just someone who finally did something impractical. Probably too late. Definitely too expensive." She met his eyes. "That's all I am."

Senn studied her for a long moment.

"Everyone on this train is a suspect, Ms. Quinn," he said finally. "That includes you." He stood. "You're free to go. For now."

For now.

She stayed after he left. Her hands weren't shaking. She was surprised by that. She'd expected to feel worse. Accused, cornered, undone. Instead she just felt tired. And oddly clear, the way you felt after crying, or confessing, or finally saying something you'd been holding too long.

A honey trap. At fifty. Robin would laugh herself sick.

But the absurdity didn't make it less real. Her name was in that notebook, with its own question mark. Every observation she'd written down could be read another way now. Not as habit. As reconnaissance.

She had to find out what had actually happened on this train. Not for Victoria.

For herself.

Back in her cabin, Iris picked up her phone. No signal. The fog had swallowed that too.

She typed the message anyway.

Senn thinks I was working with Victoria. I'm officially a suspect. This is going great.

It sat there, unsent. Robin would have something to say about this. Probably something practical. Possibly something beginning with *I warned you* and ending with *get home.*

Iris set the phone down and reached for her journal.

I am a suspect.

She looked at the words for a long moment.

In the books, the wrongly accused person usually had something compelling about them. A secret history. A dramatic motive. A reason that made narrative sense.

She had a handkerchief and unfortunate timing.

She flipped back a few pages.

Victoria was a con artist. Professional. Richard fit the profile—older, wealthy, alone. But Victoria had been working Edmund, not

Richard. Why?

Unless Edmund had been a diversion.

Unless she already had Richard.

Iris paused. Crossed out the line. The thought wasn't wrong, exactly. Just too tidy.

She turned the page.

The inventory from the midnight search was there, written in her small, precise hand.

Edmund: cocaine. Claimed it was planted.

Theo: cocaine, pills, other things. Admitted immediately.

Margaret: enough sleeping pills to sedate a boarding school.

Richard: heart medication, organized by day.

Danny: nothing.

Elena: Victoria's bracelet and scarf.

She underlined Danny's name. Then, after a moment, Elena's.

Con artists accumulated enemies. That alone didn't narrow things down.

Iris closed the journal and stared at the wall.

For twenty-three years, people had come to her with questions like riddles. *I need a book about a girl in a blue coat. It might have been winter. The title started with T. Or maybe M.*

They never gave you the right details. They gave you the ones that felt important to them. You learned to listen past that.

She opened the journal again.

Victoria had been poisoned. The poison had been in the glass before the toast. The glasses had moved. Hands everywhere. No one watching closely enough.

And she—she had been watching faces.

That was the mistake.

She let her eyes move over the pages, not reading so much as noticing: where her pen had pressed harder, where she'd circled things instead of underlining them.

Something here didn't fit. Not a missing fact. A misread one.

She didn't know whose. Or how. Or what it meant yet.

But she knew that feeling. The one you got when a book was on the right shelf and still in the wrong place.

She stood and smoothed her cardigan. The woman in the mirror looked back at her—tired, thoughtful, very likely about to make things worse.

"Well," Iris said quietly.

She'd done that before too.

14

"The secret," Danny said, "is that most people use boiling water. You shouldn't. It burns the leaves."

Iris wasn't entirely sure how she'd ended up here. The observation car, Danny Morrison explaining tea as if tea were the thing that mattered right now. Her cabin had started to close in on her—all that velvet, all that silence—and the dining car meant people. This had seemed like a reasonable third option.

"You want it just off the boil," Danny continued, pouring water into the pot. Steam rose between them. "And then you wait. Ninety seconds. Most people rush."

"I'm not really a tea person," Iris said. She'd been trying to become one for years. All those rituals, the beautiful china, the civilized appeal of it. It had never taken.

"That's because no one's taught you properly." He reached into his jacket pocket and produced a small jar. Honey, golden and thick. He'd brought his own. Of course he had.

"This is from a farm in the Cotswolds," he said, unscrewing the lid. "The bees only forage on wildflowers. You can taste the difference." He added a spoonful to her cup, stirring carefully. "The honey helps. Smooths the edges."

Iris didn't have the heart to tell him her favorite honey came in a plastic bear from the grocery store. She'd been squeezing it onto toast for decades without once considering what the bees had been foraging on.

She took a sip. It was good. Actually good. Not the bitter, watery disappointment of her usual attempts.

It still wasn't coffee. But she didn't say that.

"Well?" Danny asked.

"I'm not converted. But it's good."

He smiled like that was exactly the answer he'd expected.

For a moment, neither of them spoke. The train creaked around them. Settling sounds, the kind old buildings made.

Danny looked tired, she realized. Not the dramatic exhaustion of Edmund, who wore his suffering like a costume. This was quieter. The kind of tired that came from taking care of someone else for a long time.

"You've been looking after Richard for a while," she said. It wasn't quite a question.

"Since his diagnosis. Three years now." Danny turned his cup again. "He didn't want anyone fussing over him. Said he'd managed over seventy years without a nursemaid and wasn't about to start. But someone had to make sure he took his medications. Ate properly."

"How's he doing with all of this?"

Danny looked down at his cup. "Tired. More tired than he wants to admit."

"The search rattled him."

"The search. The questioning. All of it." Danny paused. "He feels responsible, somehow. Even though it has nothing to do with him."

"Why would he feel responsible?"

"That's Richard. He takes things on. Other people's troubles." Danny's voice had softened, the way it did when he talked about his uncle. "He's been like that since I was a boy. Always trying to fix things. Even things that aren't his to fix. Or aren't fixable."

Iris thought about Richard at dinner that first night. The way he'd listened to Mrs. Winslow's stories about Herbert. The way he'd included Iris without making her feel like charity. Some people had that gift, making space for others without seeming to try.

"Senn questioned him for a long time yesterday," Danny said. "Longer than anyone else, I think."

"Why?"

Danny was quiet for a moment. When he spoke again, his voice was careful.

"Apparently they'd crossed paths before. Richard and Victoria. Some event in London, a year ago. Donors and patrons—you know how those things are."

Iris didn't, actually. But she nodded.

"Richard barely remembered her. One conversation at a crowded party—he meets hundreds of people at those things. But Senn wanted every detail. Every word exchanged."

Danny shook his head.

"As if anyone could recall a five-minute conversation from a year ago."

"Could he? Recall it?"

"Some of it. She'd asked about his work. Investment opportunities." Danny looked at his tea. "At the time, he thought she was just making conversation. Now, of course—"

He didn't finish. He didn't need to.

Victoria had been working. Even then. Identifying marks, gathering information, filing wealthy men away for future use. And Richard had been on her list.

Iris thought about what Senn had told her. Con artist. Professional. Targeted wealthy older men.

Richard was wealthy. Richard was older. Richard was exactly her type.

She tried to imagine it. Victoria at some glittering charity event, champagne in hand, scanning the room the way a librarian scanned the stacks. Looking for what she needed, assessing what was available. And there was Richard, kind and wealthy and recently widowed. Still learning how to be alone.

He would have been easy. That was the terrible thing. The very qualities that made Richard good—his openness, his willingness to listen, his instinct to help—were exactly what made him vulnerable.

"Does Senn think Richard was involved?" she asked.

"Senn thinks everyone was involved. That's his job." Danny's voice had gone flat. "But Richard couldn't have done this. Our cabins share a wall. I would have heard him leave. I didn't."

Iris wrapped her hands around her teacup.

She thought about the night Victoria died. The chaos in the corridor. Margaret screaming at Howard. Edmund pounding on doors. The whole train awake and stumbling over each other in the dark.

And Richard's voice, cutting through all of it: *For the love of God, would everyone please just shut up and go to bed?*

That had been around two-thirty. She'd heard him clearly. Which meant she'd heard him in the corridor. Not in his cabin. In the corridor, same as the rest of them.

She didn't say anything. Just turned her cup in her hands.

"I keep thinking about Theo," Danny said.

The shift surprised her. "Theo?"

"The way he watched everyone that first night. Victoria especially."

Danny leaned back.

"I don't know. Something about him bothers me. All those drawings, all that watching. But you never learn anything about him in return."

Iris thought about Theo. The fox pajamas. The cocaine. The wink in the corridor.

"He's private," she said.

"Private." Danny nodded slowly. "That's one word for it."

"You think he's hiding something?"

"I don't know. Maybe I'm just tired and looking for someone to blame." He rubbed his eyes. "Forget I said anything." He stood, brushing something invisible from his sleeve. "I should check on Richard. He doesn't like to be alone too long these days."

"Thank you. For the tea."

"Any time." He paused at the door. "Iris. Be careful, will you? Until this is all sorted out."

"Careful of what?"

"Everyone." A small smile. "We're all just strangers here."

Then he was gone and the observation car was quiet.

Outside, the afternoon light had gone flat and gray. She wasn't sure what time it was anymore. The days had started to blur together. Meals and interrogations and conversations that felt like interrogations even when they weren't.

Iris sat with her cup. The honey sweetness lingered on her tongue.

Danny had been kind. He was always kind. Helping Richard, helping Elena, helping her now with tea she hadn't asked for. Some people were like that. They couldn't stop themselves.

But Richard had been in the corridor that night. At two-thirty, yelling at everyone to shut up. She'd heard him clearly. And Danny had just said he never left his cabin.

Maybe Danny had been asleep. Maybe he'd misspoken. Maybe it was nothing.

And Victoria had known Richard. Had met him before, at some

party neither of them had mentioned until Senn started asking questions. One conversation, Danny said. Five minutes. Barely worth remembering.

But Victoria had remembered. Victoria, who made a living reading wealthy men and deciding which ones were worth her time.

Richard had been worth remembering.

Iris set down her cup.

Three days ago, she'd boarded this train thinking the hardest part was over. She'd made the decision. Spent the money. Shown up. All that was left was to enjoy it—the scenery, the champagne, the feeling of finally doing something she'd dreamed about for thirty-three years.

Now a woman was dead. Iris was a suspect. And the people she'd started to think of as friends were turning into question marks, one by one.

She thought about Robin, unreachable on the other side of all that fog. Robin would tell her to trust her instincts.

But Iris wasn't sure her instincts could be trusted. She'd read Victoria as a femme fatale, which was true, but she'd missed the con artist underneath. She'd read Richard as kind, which was also true, but kindness didn't mean innocence. She'd read Danny as devoted, and maybe he was, but devoted people did terrible things sometimes. To protect the people they loved.

The list in her head kept growing. Small things. Inconsistencies. The kind of details that might mean nothing or might mean everything. She couldn't stop collecting them, couldn't stop arranging them into patterns that refused to resolve.

Like a shelf of books that didn't quite fit. You couldn't always say why it bothered you. You just knew it did.

The windows showed nothing. The train sat motionless, waiting for something that hadn't come yet.

She was waiting too. She just wasn't sure for what.

15

She couldn't sleep.

She'd brought *A Room with a View* for the journey. It had seemed right when she packed it. A woman traveling, seeing new things, waking up to her own life. She'd read it six times over the years. The paperback was soft as cloth, the margins full of pencil notes from her twenties, her thirties, her forties. A record of who she'd been each time.

But tonight the words wouldn't settle. Lucy Honeychurch was in Florence, standing at a window, waiting for something to happen. Iris kept reading the same paragraph over and over. The pension. The view. The old ladies arguing about rooms.

She set the book on her chest and stared at the ceiling, began counting the brass rivets on the ceiling trim. Thirty-seven. She counted them again to be sure.

At home, when she couldn't sleep, she'd pace the apartment while Fable watched from the couch, blinking slowly, as if to say: *this is a you problem.*

By midnight, staying still had become unbearable. She put on the robe and stepped into the corridor.

She'd expected relief. Movement, at least, even if it was just her own.

Instead, the corridor felt wrong

Not in any way she could point to. The brass still gleamed. The carpet still swallowed her footsteps. But the quality of the silence had changed. It was thicker now, and watchful. The sconce lights cast pools of amber that didn't quite reach each other, leaving dark between.

Somewhere behind her, a door clicked. Soft. Deliberate.

She didn't turn to see which one.

Gothic novel, she thought. *The one where the heroine shouldn't be wandering alone at night.*

Iris wandered anyway.

She passed the Ashfords' door. Dark, but she could hear Howard snoring through the wood. It was a thick, wet rattle. Decades of listening to that sound. No wonder Margaret looked at him that way during meals.

She passed Theo's door. Also dark. She slowed without meaning to, listening for the scratch of pencil on paper, the creak of a chair. Heard nothing.

She passed Victoria's door. The yellow tape made a crooked X across the frame. Someone had already started to peel back one corner, whether from carelessness or curiosity she couldn't tell.

Ahead was the bar car.

It had been intimidating her since London. She'd passed it several times, glancing through the glass the way she glanced at restaurant menus posted outside places she'd never enter. It glowed. Amber and polished and full of people who knew which gin to order.

She pushed the door open.

It was much smaller than she'd expected. Dark wood, green leather, bottles arranged behind the bar with the care of a museum exhibit. Everything gleamed. The brass fittings, the crystal glasses, the leather chairs that probably cost more than her sofa. This was a room that had been beautiful in 1920 and had been kept beautiful ever since—not preserved like a relic, but maintained like a promise.

This is what travel used to mean. This is what it still means, if you can afford it.

Photographs lined one wall. Not yellowed, not faded. Restored, probably, or replaced with archival prints. Passengers from another era. Women in silk, men in evening dress. The Orient Express in its first life, when the journey to Istanbul took diplomats and aristocrats and people who thought nothing of crossing a continent for dinner.

Iris wondered what they'd talked about in this room. What secrets had been traded over whiskey, what lies had been told, what deals had been made. A hundred years of people passing through, leaving nothing behind but the faint impression of having been somewhere that mattered.

Theo, to her surprise, sat still at a corner table.

She thought about turning around. Going back to her cabin to count the brass rivets on the ceiling again.

There was a bottle on the table and a glass in his hand. No scarf. No sketchbook. Just him and the whiskey and that wall of white nothing where the Alps should have been.

He looked up. "Ms. Quinn. Couldn't sleep either? It seems that no one sleeps on the Orient Express."

"I was looking for the library car," she lied.

"Library's the other direction."

He gestured at the chair across from him. "But you're welcome to the alternative."

Against her better judgment, she crossed the room and sat. The leather was cold.

Theo poured whiskey into an empty glass and slid it toward her.

Her hand didn't move.

"Not poisoned," he said. He poured more into his own glass and drank. "If it were, I wouldn't be drinking it."

"Comforting."

She picked up the glass. Took the smallest sip. It burned.

For a while, neither of them spoke.

"You know the worst part?" Theo finally said, staring at something unseen. "It's not being a suspect. It's knowing whoever actually did kill Victoria is somewhere on this train right now. Probably sleeping fine."

"You think they're sleeping fine?"

"People like that usually do."

He poured more whiskey. His movements were looser now.

"They've already justified it to themselves. Convinced themselves someone deserved it. After that, the rest is easy."

"That's a very specific theory."

"I've known a lot of people who were good at justifying things." He turned the glass in his hand. "My father, for one. Could talk himself into anything. Talk anyone else into it too, if he needed to. It's a skill. I never inherited it."

"What did you inherit?"

"Money." He said it flat, like a fact that bored him. "And the nose. Grandmother's side. She never forgave me for it."

Iris waited. People usually kept talking if you didn't fill the silence. Librarian trick. It worked on Theo too.

"Creativity, I suppose." He shrugged. "My father was an actor. I was always in the wings, taking notes."

"Edmund thinks he's being framed," she said. "The cocaine."

"Edmund thinks a lot of things." Theo shrugged. "Doesn't make them true."

"You don't like him."

"It's nothing personal." He drained his glass. "Edmund's just louder about his problems than most people. Makes him easy to dismiss. But that doesn't mean he's wrong about everything."

He poured more whiskey. Stared at it. "Do you think she knew?" He asked, his eyes now steady, locked on hers.

Iris didn't have to ask who.

"Knew what?"

"That someone wanted her dead." He was looking at the fog again. "That night, at dinner. The champagne. Did she have any idea what was coming? Or did she just think it was another evening, another room full of people looking at her, same as always?"

It was a strange question. The kind you asked when you'd been thinking about someone too much.

"I don't know," Iris said.

"No." He turned his glass. "I suppose you wouldn't."

"It's late. I'm drunk." He stood, caught himself on the chair, overcorrected. The whiskey bottle was nearly empty now—she hadn't noticed him refilling, but he must have been at it before she arrived. "Get some sleep. If you can."

He made it to the door on the second try. Didn't look back. The door slid shut behind him.

Iris sat in the quiet, her whiskey going warm in her hand. She should go back to her cabin.

She was about to stand when she saw it.

The sketchbook. Tucked into the corner of his chair, half-hidden by the cushion. He must have set it down when she came in and forgotten it.

She stared at it.

Don't, said fifty years of professionalism. The voice of a woman who had never once looked at a patron's borrowing history. Who had protected the privacy of every nervous teenager checking out books about things they weren't ready to discuss with their parents.

She picked it up anyway.

The cover was worn soft, the binding loose from years of use. Not a new sketchbook bought for this trip. This was something he'd been carrying for a while. She opened it carefully, the way she'd open any book that had been loved hard. The spine cracked slightly. The pages were thick, creamy, the kind of paper that cost real money. Pencil smudges on the edges where his hand had rested.

No dates. No captions. Just the drawings.

The first pages weren't from the train. A cafe somewhere, wrought-iron chairs, a waiter with a towel over his arm. A street scene, European, cobblestones and shuttered windows.

A woman sleeping, her face half-buried in a pillow. Intimate in a way that made Iris feel like she was intruding. She turned past that one quickly.

Then the train.

Margaret first. Not cruel. Just Margaret, captured in graphite. The set of her jaw, the pearls, the posture. But Theo had seen something else, something in her eyes that looked almost like fear. Iris wouldn't have drawn it that way. She'd seen Margaret as formidable. Impenetrable.

She turned the page.

Howard. Slumped, staring at nothing. Multiple studies of him on the same page. Howard from different angles, different moments. As if Theo had kept returning to him, trying to get something right. In one sketch, Howard's hand was on his wedding ring, twisting it. Iris hadn't noticed him doing that. But now that she saw it drawn, she realized she had. She just hadn't registered it as meaning anything.

Edmund. Reciting his poem, one hand raised. But also: Edmund alone at a window, his face crumpled into something almost human. And in the corner of that page, small, barely more than a gesture—Edmund looking at Victoria. The angle of his body. The want in it, reduced to a few lines. Theo had seen that too. Seen it and immortalized it.

Then there was Mrs. Winslow. Just one drawing, but perfect. Serene. Her hands folded in her lap, joyful eyes on something outside the frame. She looked like a woman who had outlived everyone who might have surprised her.

The page after was Danny and Richard. The warmth between them. But Iris noticed something else: Danny's hand, resting on Richard's arm. It was drawn with more pressure than the rest. The lines darker, more deliberate. As if Theo had traced over them. As if that detail mattered.

Elena pouring tea. Her face in profile, her posture careful. Professional. But her shoulders were tight. Theo had caught that too—the tension she carried. The bracing.

The elderly couple from car three, holding hands across a table. A steward adjusting a lamp. Mountains dissolving into fog.

And then herself.

She stopped.

It was her. Sitting at a window in the observation car, her reflection ghosted in the glass, her face turned toward something outside the frame.

She didn't look the way she looked in mirrors. In mirrors she saw the things that needed fixing. The hair, the posture, the general dishevelment of a woman who had stopped trying. This was different. The lines were gentle.

She looked sad. She looked like she was waiting for something she didn’t expect would come.

When had he drawn this? She'd sat in the observation car a dozen times. Hadn’t remembered feeling that way. Looking that way.

She turned the page. And the next. And the next.

Empty. Blank pages waiting.

She went back through from the beginning. The cafe, the

street scene, the sleeping woman. Then the train. Margaret. Howard. Edmund. Mrs. Winslow. Richard. Danny. Elena. The landscapes. Herself.

Everyone.

Everyone except Victoria.

The most striking woman on the train.

The woman every eye had followed from the moment she'd stepped aboard. The woman Theo had just asked about, unprompted, his voice strange in the dark—*did she have any idea what was coming?*

Iris sat very still.

The bar door opened.

She looked up.

Theo was standing in the doorway. His eyes went to the sketchbook in her hands. His jaw tightened. The color left his face.

"That's mine." Flat. Controlled.

"You left it—"

"Give it to me."

He crossed the room in three strides and took it from her hands before she could react.

"I'm sorry," Iris said. "I shouldn't have—"

"No. You shouldn't have."

He looked at her. Just for a moment. Anger, yes. But underneath it, fear. The look of a man caught at something he couldn't explain.

Then he left.

Iris sat alone in the bar car.

She'd categorized him wrong. Not literary fiction at all. Not the detached observer, watching humanity from an ironic distance. This was something else. *Psychological thriller,* maybe. *The kind where the narrator tells you everything except the one thing that matters.*

She tried to remember exactly what she'd seen. The order of

the pages. Margaret first, then Howard, then Edmund. Had there been sketches she'd turned too quickly?

She couldn't be sure. And now the book was gone.

You didn't not-draw someone by accident. Not when you drew everyone else. Not when she'd been the most visible person on the train.

The corridor was silent when she stepped out. She walked back toward her compartment. Passed Richard and Danny's doors, dark and quiet. Passed Theo's.

Light under his door. A thin yellow line.

She stopped.

He was in there right now. The sketchbook open in his lap, probably. Paging through to see what she might have seen. Wondering how much she knew and what she'd do with it.

She'd seen plenty.

16

Iris was halfway to Senn's compartment before she talked herself out of it.

She'd been so certain at six in the morning, lying awake with the discovery still fresh. A missing person. A hole in the record. The kind of absence that meant something. By six-fifteen she was dressed. By six-thirty she was in the corridor, rehearsing what she'd say.

By six-forty-five she'd stopped walking.

What did she actually have? A sketchbook she shouldn't have opened. A woman who wasn't drawn. And Theo's face when he'd caught her—angry, yes, but something else underneath. Fear, maybe. Or just the raw exposure of being seen.

She could hear Robin's voice: *You broke into his private things and now you want to report him for not drawing someone?*

She hadn't broken in. He'd left it behind.

Semantics, Robin would say. *You still looked.*

She had. And she wasn't sorry. But standing in the corridor at quarter to seven, the certainty that had propelled her out of bed was starting to thin. Senn would ask questions. How did you come to see the sketchbook? Why were you in the bar car at midnight? Why did you keep looking once you realized what it was?

She didn't have good answers. She had the same answer she'd had for everything on this trip: *Because I wanted to. Because I was tired of not doing things.*

That wasn't going to impress a Swiss police inspector.

She turned around and went to breakfast instead.

THE DINING CAR SMELLED LIKE COFFEE AND PERFORMANCE. EVERYONE working very hard to seem normal. Forks scraping china. Murmured conversations that stopped when footsteps approached. The Orient Express, determined to pretend the last several days had been a minor inconvenience rather than a complete derailment of everyone's holiday plans.

Iris admired the commitment. It was the same energy as the library's annual report, the one that described "challenges in patron engagement" instead of "that man who screamed at Janet about late fees until security came."

She didn't look for Theo's corner. She already knew it would be empty.

Richard caught her eye from across the room and raised his coffee cup—half greeting, half summons. Danny was already pulling out the chair beside him.

"—completely unreasonable," Danny was saying as she sat down. "The altitude alone—"

"The altitude is fine. I've been to the Alps before."

"Not recently. Not with your—"

"My what?" Richard's voice had an edge. "Finish the sentence."

Danny didn't finish the sentence. He poured tea instead, the gesture tight with things unsaid.

"Good morning, Iris." Richard turned to her with the particular warmth of a man grateful for interruption. "Please tell my nephew that a short walk in the mountains is not a death sentence."

"I didn't say death sentence. I said inadvisable."

"You said inadvisable in a tone that meant death sentence."

Iris opened her mouth. Closed it. She had something to tell them—something important—but they were already moving on.

"The doctor in Zurich said moderate exercise," Danny continued. "Moderate. A walk through alpine terrain at elevation is not—"

"The doctor in Zurich has never seen an alpine meadow in his life. The man thinks nature is a potted fern in a waiting room."

"He thinks nature is irrelevant to cardiac function, which it is."

"Everything is relevant to cardiac function. That's rather the point of having a heart."

Elena appeared with coffee. Iris took the cup gratefully, wrapping her hands around it, waiting for an opening.

"When we get to Istanbul," Richard said, "I intend to walk up to the Galata Tower. All the way up. Every step."

"There's a lift."

"I don't want the lift. I want the steps."

"You want to prove something."

"I want to see the view. The view one earns. There's a difference."

Danny made a sound that wasn't quite agreement.

"Actually—" Iris began.

"And another thing," Richard said, turning to her as if she'd been part of the conversation all along. "He's been reading my medication bottles. I caught him this morning, holding one up to the light like a suspicious pharmacist."

"I was checking the dosage."

"You were counting pills. I saw you."

"Because you don't always—" Danny stopped. Took a breath. "Fine. I was counting pills. Because last week you forgot your evening dose twice, and you didn't tell me until—"

"I didn't tell you because it wasn't relevant."

"Wasn't relevant? Your heart medication wasn't—"

"I remembered eventually. That's what matters."

Iris took a sip of coffee. They were talking across her now, the argument worn smooth by repetition. She recognized the shape of it—the same fight they'd probably been having for years, the words changing but the music staying the same.

"I found something," she said.

Neither of them heard her.

"—can't keep track of everything myself," Danny was saying. "I'm not asking for much. Just a system. A simple—"

"I have a system."

"Taking pills when you remember isn't a system."

"It's worked for seventy-five years."

"It hasn't worked. That's exactly my point. Your heart—"

"My heart is my business."

"Your heart is literally my business. I'm a cardiac surgeon."

"Not my cardiac surgeon."

"No, because you won't let me—"

"Because you're my nephew, not my doctor, and there are boundaries—"

"There's something I need to tell you," Iris said, louder this time.

They both stopped. Turned to her. The argument hung in the air between them, unfinished.

"Sorry," Danny said. He had the grace to look embarrassed. "We're doing it again."

"Bickering like an old married couple," Richard agreed. "It's unbecoming. Please, Iris. What is it?"

Now she had the opening, she wasn't sure where to start.

"Last night," she said. "I couldn't sleep. I went to the bar car."

"Understandable," Richard said. "I've considered it myself."

"Theo was there."

Something shifted in Danny's expression. Subtle, but there.

"We talked. He'd been drinking. When he left, he forgot his sketchbook."

She paused. This was the part where she'd done something wrong. Where she'd crossed a line she couldn't uncross.

"I looked."

Richard nodded slowly. No judgment in his face. Just listening.

"And?" Danny asked.

"Everyone's in it. Pages of us. Margaret, Howard, Edmund, Mrs. Winslow. Elena. The landscapes. Even me." She set down her coffee cup. "Everyone except Victoria."

The table went quiet.

Danny's hand had stopped halfway to his tea. Richard was very still.

"Not once?" Richard asked.

"Not a line. I went through it twice."

Danny sat back. She could see him working through it—the same process she'd gone through in the dark hours of the morning, turning the absence over and over.

"The woman every eye followed," he said slowly. "The woman who made sure every eye followed. And he never drew her."

"No."

Richard picked up his coffee. Set it down without drinking. Picked it up again.

"That's not nothing," he said finally.

"It might be nothing. It might be—I don't know. Maybe he

found her difficult. Maybe he didn't like her face. Maybe there's an explanation I haven't thought of."

"Maybe," Danny said. His voice had gone flat. "Or maybe you can't draw someone you're trying not to see."

Iris thought about Theo in the bar car. The whiskey. The question he'd asked, unprompted, his voice strange in the dark.

Did she know? That someone wanted her dead?

"He asked about her," she said. "Before I found the sketchbook. He wanted to know if she'd had any idea what was coming. Whether she'd understood, at the end."

Richard and Danny exchanged a look. The kind of look that held a whole conversation.

"Tell Senn," Richard said.

"It feels thin. A missing sketch. A strange question. It's not evidence."

"It's a thread." Richard's voice was firm now. Decided. "And right now, you're still the one Senn keeps circling back to. The handkerchief. The savings. Give him someone else to look at."

"He's right," Danny said. "Whatever this means—whatever Theo was or wasn't doing—Senn needs to hear it. Let him decide if it matters."

Iris looked at the two of them. Richard, who was dying and didn't want to talk about it. Danny, who was watching him die and couldn't stop talking about it. Both of them looking at her like she'd done something right.

"All right," she said. "I'll tell him."

"After you eat something." Danny pushed the bread basket toward her. "You look like you slept about as well as I did."

"I didn't sleep at all."

"Then you definitely need toast."

There was a silver rack beside the basket—four half-slices standing upright in their own little slots, each piece perfectly vertical, like toast had finally found its dignity. She'd never seen one before. She hadn't known this was what toast needed, but it was.

She took a piece. Bit into it without tasting it.

Somewhere on this train, Theo was looking at his sketchbook, wondering what she'd seen. Somewhere on this train, Senn was making notes in his careful hand, adding evidence to columns, drawing lines between names.

And here she was, eating toast, about to walk into an interrogation and point at someone else.

The bread was good. She made herself notice that. Made herself be here, in this moment, with these people who'd made room for her.

Then she set down the toast and stood.

"Wish me luck," she said.

"Luck," Richard said.

Danny just nodded. But his eyes followed her as she walked away, and she felt the weight of it all the way to the door.

17

The walk to Senn's compartment felt longer than it should have.

She'd made this trip before—twice now, both times dreading what waited at the other end. But this was different. She wasn't being summoned. She was choosing to go. Choosing to point at someone and say *look here, not at me.*

The corridor stretched ahead of her. Brass fittings, walnut panels, that carpet that swallowed footsteps. She'd walked this corridor a dozen times now. At some point it had stopped feeling like the Orient Express and started feeling like the hallway outside her supervisor's office—the one she'd traveled every year for performance reviews, rehearsing what she'd say, knowing she'd say something else entirely.

She stopped outside his door. Raised her hand to knock.

You don't have to do this, Robin's voice said. *You could turn around. Go back to your cabin. Let Senn figure it out himself.*

But Senn wasn't figuring it out himself. Senn was figuring her out—her savings, her handkerchief, her convenient presence in all the wrong places. If she didn't give him another direction, he'd keep walking the same one.

She knocked.

"Come in."

Senn was writing when she entered. He finished his sentence before looking up—a small assertion of control, deliberate and obvious. She was learning his rhythms now. The silences, the waiting, the way he let you hang yourself with your own words if you talked too much.

The chair was in the same position. The window let in the same flat light. She was getting tired of this room the way you got tired of a book you'd been assigned to read—dutiful, resentful, wishing you could skip to the end and find out if it was worth it.

She sat without being invited. That felt like progress.

"Ms. Quinn." He set down his pen. "I didn't expect to see you again so soon."

"I have information. About Theo Mercer."

Something shifted in his expression. Subtle, but there. Interest, maybe. Or just the particular attention of a man whose job was listening.

"Go on."

She told him. The bar car. The whiskey. The sketchbook left behind.

"I shouldn't have looked," she said. "But I did."

Senn didn't respond to that. Didn't absolve her or condemn her. Just waited.

"He's been drawing since we boarded. Everyone—passengers, staff, landscapes. Pages and pages of us. I'm in there. So is everyone else." She paused. "Except Victoria."

"Explain."

"She's not in the sketchbook. Not once. Not a sketch, not a study, not even a gesture." Iris leaned forward slightly. "An artist who draws compulsively, who can't stop recording faces—and he never once put pencil to paper for the woman who worked hardest to be seen? That's not oversight. That's intention."

Senn picked up his pen. Made a note. From where she sat, she could see fragments—a name that started with T, a word that might have been *connection*, a date she couldn't quite make out.

"He came back for it," she continued. "The sketchbook. He'd left it behind, and when he realized I had it—" She remembered his face. The anger, yes. But something else underneath. "He was afraid. Not embarrassed. Afraid."

"Did he say anything?"

"He took it and left. But before that, in the bar, he asked me something strange. About Victoria. Whether she'd known what was coming. Whether she'd understood, at the end."

Senn's pen stopped moving.

"Those were his words? 'Whether she'd understood, at the end'?"

"Close enough. He was drunk. But that was the meaning."

Silence. The train creaked around them—that settling sound it made when stopped too long, like joints stiffening.

Senn closed his notebook. When he looked at her again, something in his posture had changed. The interrogator replaced by something else. Someone about to share information instead of extract it.

"Ms. Quinn. The background inquiries have produced results."

She waited.

"Theo Mercer and Victoria Halberstam have financial connections. Joint accounts. Transfers between them going back two years."

The words landed slowly. She turned them over, fitting them against what she knew. Theo watching Victoria at dinner. The careful distance between them. The way they'd never spoken, never acknowledged each other.

Not strangers avoiding each other.

Partners pretending to be strangers.

"He was her scout," Iris said. It wasn't a question. "He watched people. Noticed things. Reported back."

"A reasonable inference."

"And she was cutting him out." That part came slower, piecing itself together as she spoke. "The withdrawals you mentioned. She was taking money. Leaving."

Senn neither confirmed nor denied. But his silence had a shape to it—the shape of someone who'd reached the same conclusion.

"You are cleared, Ms. Quinn."

The words arrived without ceremony. No fanfare. No apology for the days of suspicion, the questions, the handkerchief in its evidence bag.

"The financial connection explains the elements that required explanation," Senn continued. "Your presence in the corridor that night. The handkerchief. Your observations." Almost a smile. Almost. "You were simply an unfortunate bystander with inconvenient timing."

She should feel relieved. She'd imagined this moment—the weight lifting, the suspicion dissolving, the triumphant return to her cabin where she'd pour herself a drink and call Robin and say *I told you I didn't do it.*

Instead she felt unmoored. Like finishing a book you'd been dreading and realizing you had no idea what to do with your afternoon.

Iris Quinn: no longer a murder suspect. She'd have to update her resume.

"What happens now?"

Senn stood. "Now we make an arrest."

She walked back to her cabin slowly. No one stopped her. No one asked where she was going. She was just a passenger again—

a woman on a train, going somewhere, no longer interesting enough to watch.

She should be grateful for that. She'd spent fifty years cultivating invisibility. It was disorienting to realize she'd almost miss being seen.

In her cabin, she sat on the edge of the bed.

The velvet was familiar now. She'd stopped noticing how expensive it was, how absurd—marble bathrooms on a moving train, like something from a fever dream. It was just where she lived now. The way the library had become just where she worked, somewhere between her fifth year and her fifteenth, the wonder worn down to routine.

She thought about calling Robin. But what would she say? *I solved a murder. Or helped solve one. Or pointed at someone until someone else solved it.* None of those sounded right. None of them sounded like her.

She thought about Theo. The fox pajamas. The wink in the corridor. The way he'd watched everyone, sketched everyone, seen everything.

Not everything. He hadn't seen this coming. Or maybe he had, and that's why he'd been drinking alone in the bar car at midnight, asking strange questions about dead women.

Did she know? That someone wanted her dead?

Had he been asking about Victoria? Or about himself?

The commotion came an hour later.

Footsteps first—heavy, official, the kind that didn't belong on a train where everything was designed to move quietly. Then voices, low and firm. Iris was at her door before she'd decided to move, some instinct pulling her toward the sound.

The corridor was narrow. From her doorway, she could see them clearly—two officers flanking Theo's door, Senn standing to the side with that patient expression she was beginning to understand meant nothing and everything at once.

Theo's door opened.

He emerged in handcuffs. His wrists looked thin in them, almost delicate. He was wearing the scarf—the artfully knotted one she'd noticed that first day on the platform, when she'd filed him under *literary fiction* and thought she understood what that meant.

She'd been wrong about the genre. She'd been wrong about a lot of things.

Though to be fair, *literary fiction turning out to be crime thriller* wasn't the most dramatic genre shift she'd witnessed this week. That honor went to Victoria, who'd gone from *femme fatale* to *victim* without any of the usual foreshadowing.

The officers guided him forward. The corridor was narrow. She could have stepped back. Closed the door. Let him pass. She should look away. Give him his dignity. That's what people did.

She didn't look away.

Theo's eyes found hers.

He stopped walking. Just for a second—just long enough for the officers' grip to tighten, for the rhythm of the procession to break.

His face wasn't what she expected. Not guilt. Not defeat. Not the resignation of a man who'd been caught.

Surprise. Genuine, unguarded surprise. Like someone who'd opened a door expecting one room and found another entirely.

"The sketchbook," he said. His voice was flat. Emptied. "You told him about the sketchbook."

She didn't answer. Couldn't.

"I never drew her." He was still looking at her, and something in his eyes made her want to step back, press harder into the wall. "I couldn't. Every time I tried—"

"Mr. Mercer." Senn's voice, quiet and final.

The officers pulled him forward. Two steps. Three. Then he twisted back, fighting their grip, and his eyes found hers again.

"The murderer is still on this train."

Then he was gone. Through the door, down the steps, out into whatever waited.

Iris stood very still.

The murderer is still on this train.

He'd said it like he believed it. Like he needed her to believe it too.

But Senn had evidence. Bank records. Joint accounts. A motive that made sense now—the partner being cut out, the money disappearing, the woman who'd used him deciding she didn't need him anymore. The empty pages in the sketchbook. You didn't draw the person you were hiding your connection to. You kept that space blank, that evidence absent.

It made sense.

It all made sense.

The murderer is still on this train.

She was still hearing it three hours later, when Danny found her in the observation car.

"They're gone," he said. "Senn and his people. The train leaves in twenty minutes."

"I know."

He sat down across from her. Outside the window, the fog had finally begun to lift. She could see shapes now—mountains emerging like something remembered, like a photograph developing in reverse.

"You solved it," Danny said. "You noticed what no one else noticed. How are you feeling?"

How was she feeling? She'd been asking herself that for hours.

"I don't know," she said honestly. "Relieved, I suppose."

"But?"

Of course there was a but. Danny noticed things too.

"He looked surprised," she said. "When they took him. Not caught. Not guilty. Surprised."

"Shock. Denial. Criminals convince themselves they won't be caught, and when they are—" Danny shrugged. "It takes time to accept."

"Maybe."

"Iris." He leaned forward, and his voice was gentle. "You found the evidence. Senn confirmed it—financial connections going back years. Theo was her partner. Motive, means, opportunity. It's over."

She nodded. It was over. Everyone kept saying so.

"Richard wants to celebrate," Danny continued. "Dinner tonight. The three of us. He's already made arrangements with the kitchen—special wine, the whole production. He's absurdly pleased about it." A smile. "What do you say?"

The train lurched. A shudder, then movement—actual movement, after all these days of stillness. The dream she'd spent her savings on, finally continuing.

"Dinner sounds nice," she said.

Danny's smile widened. That warm, easy smile she'd liked since the first day. The smile of a man who took care of people.

"Good. Get some rest before then. You've earned it."

He stood. Squeezed her shoulder once—brief, warm—and walked away.

The observation car was empty now. Just Iris and the windows and the mountains finally showing themselves.

She should feel relieved. She'd been suspected and cleared. She'd noticed what no one else noticed. She'd helped catch a killer.

So why did she feel like someone who'd finished a book only to realize the last chapter was missing?

Robin would tell her to stop. Enjoy the wine. Enjoy the dinner. Stop looking for problems where problems had already been solved.

Robin wasn't here.

Iris pulled out her journal. Opened it to a blank page. Stared at it for a long time.

She didn't write anything.

She just sat there, watching the mountains emerge from the fog. Waiting for the shape of whatever she'd missed to finally show itself.

18

Dinner was fine. The wine was good. Richard told stories about deals gone wrong in Monaco that made her laugh despite herself, and Danny added corrections that made Richard wave his hand dismissively, and for two hours it felt like the kind of evening she'd imagined when she'd booked this trip.

Almost.

The train had been moving for hours now. She could feel it in her bones, that forward momentum she'd missed during the days they'd sat frozen in the Alps. Through the dining car windows, the mountains had finally emerged from the fog. Massive and moonlit, sliding past like a procession of ancient things that didn't care about murder investigations or arrested artists or women who couldn't quite believe the case was closed.

She'd smiled at the right moments. Raised her glass when Richard toasted. Laughed at Danny's impression of a Swiss customs official. Performed "woman having a lovely evening" well enough that no one asked if she was okay.

But underneath all of it, Theo's face kept surfacing. That look. Not guilt. Surprise.

The murderer is still on this train.

She went to bed at eleven. Lay there until one, watching shadows move across the velvet canopy. The rhythm of the tracks should have been soothing. It wasn't.

At one-fifteen, she gave up and put on the robe again. At this point, she'd worn it more than anything else she'd brought.

The corridor was empty. Dimmed for night, the brass fixtures turned down to a soft glow that made everything look like a photograph of itself. Her slippers made no sound on the carpet. The train swayed gently, and she swayed with it, one hand trailing along the wall for balance.

The library car was two carriages down. She'd grab a book, find somewhere quiet to read, and maybe by the time she finished a chapter her brain would finally agree to be quiet.

The selection was smaller than she remembered. Someone had taken the Hemingway. The Christie was back on the shelf—she wasn't touching that one again. She could still feel Senn's eyes on her, that first morning, holding Murder on the Orient Express like a confession.

She settled on an Edith Wharton. The Age of Innocence. Safe. No murders. No trains. Just repressed aristocrats making each other miserable in drawing rooms. That seemed about right.

The observation car would be empty at this hour. She could curl up by the window, watch the mountains in the dark, pretend she was the kind of person who read Wharton for pleasure instead of the kind of person who couldn't stop hearing a man say *the murderer is still on this train.*

Richard was there.

He sat alone by the window, a glass of something amber on the small table beside him. No book. No papers. Just him and the darkness outside and whatever he was thinking about.

He looked up when she came in. Didn't seem surprised. Didn't seem anything, really. Just looked at her the way you look at someone when you've already made peace with being interrupted.

"Couldn't sleep either?"

"Apparently not." She hesitated in the doorway. "I can go. If you want to be alone."

"I've had three hours of alone. Sit."

She sat. The chair was velvet, of course, cold at first, then warm. Through the window, the Alps were putting on a show. Peaks catching moonlight. Valleys pooling with shadow. The kind of view you were supposed to photograph, except she'd left her phone in the cabin, and anyway, some things you couldn't capture. You just had to look at them and know you'd never quite remember how it felt.

"Danny finally asleep?" she asked.

"No, but he hovers." Richard picked up his glass, didn't drink from it. "He thinks I don't notice. I notice."

"He worries about you."

"He does. More than he should." Richard turned the glass in his hand. "It's a strange thing, being watched that closely. You feel the weight of their fear. Every meal becomes a negotiation. Every cough, a potential crisis. After a while, you start pretending you feel better than you do, just to give them a rest."

"That sounds lonely."

"It is." He said it simply. Not complaining. Just saying. "The loneliest part of dying isn't the dying. It's pretending you're not."

Iris felt that land in her chest, like something folding in on itself.

The word sat there between them. Dying. He'd said it the way you'd say Tuesday or rain. Like it was just a fact. Like facts were all any of us had.

She'd had him wrong from the beginning, she realized.

She'd met him at tea that first day and filed him under family saga patriarch. Silver hair, kind eyes, the watch that stayed in families. The type whose role was to dispense wisdom and die at the act break, setting the inheritance plot in motion. Important to everyone else's story. Never quite the point of his own.

She hadn't understood that he was the protagonist of his own story. One that was ending.

Sitting here now, watching him turn an empty glass in his hands, she couldn't find a genre for him at all. Just a man at the end of something, trying to make sure it meant something.

"Richard—"

"My heart." He touched his chest, lightly. "Same thing that took Eleanor. The irony isn't lost on me. She spent forty years as a cardiologist, telling other people how to take care of their hearts, and then hers just—stopped. Now mine's doing the same thing. The doctors gave me months. Maybe a year if I'm careful. Which —" A short laugh. "I've never been careful about anything."

She didn't reach for the usual words. *I'm sorry. That's terrible. Is there anything I can do.* They felt too small.

“Danny doesn't want me to talk about it," Richard continued. "He thinks if we don't say it, it won't be real. But it's real. It's been real since the diagnosis. And I refuse to spend whatever time I have left pretending otherwise."

"How long have you known?"

"Long enough to stop being angry. Long enough to start thinking about what happens after."

After. Such a small word for such a big thing.

"The foundation," she said.

"Part of it." He set down his glass. "I've had a successful life, Iris. By any measure that matters to the world. Money. Influence. The right people at the right parties saying the right things about me." He paused. "And now I'm seventy-four years old, sitting on a train in the middle of the night, wondering if any of it mattered."

"Did it?"

"Some of it. The work that actually helped people. The relationships that were actually real."

He was quiet for a moment.

"Do you know what I regret?"

She shook her head.

"Not the failures. Not the deals that fell through or the money I lost. I regret the things I postponed." He leaned back in his chair. "Eleanor and I talked about spending a summer in Tuscany. Really being there. Not a vacation, but a life. Cooking, walking, learning how the days moved in a place like that." He smiled, but it didn't quite reach his eyes. "We never went. There was always a reason. Work, money, timing. And then Eleanor was gone, and I was sixty-seven, and we'd never had that summer."

“You can still go. With Danny. There's still time."

"There's always still time, until there isn't." He shifted to face her more fully. "I built things my whole life. Companies, portfolios, a reputation. All of it pointed toward some future version of myself who would finally get to enjoy it. And now—" He gestured vaguely at himself, at the train, at the night outside. "Here I am. In the future. And I'm not sure that man ever showed up."

Outside, a light appeared briefly. A village, maybe. Someone else's life, glimpsed and gone.

"I spent my savings on this trip," Iris said. She hadn't planned to say it. "Forty-eight thousand dollars. Everything I had."

Richard's eyebrow went up.

"I know. It's insane. I've never done anything impractical in my entire life." She pulled the robe tighter. "And then I turned fifty. And I found this journal I'd kept as a teenager. And I realized I'd spent thirty years waiting to become the kind of person who takes the Orient Express." She stopped. "I couldn't wait anymore."

"Good."

"Good?"

"Good." He said it with conviction. "That's exactly right."

"Most people think I'm having a breakdown."

"Most people *are* having a breakdown. They're just doing it slowly, over decades, while telling themselves they're being responsible." He picked up his glass again. "You know what I've figured out, sitting here in the dark, thinking about everything I didn't do?"

"What?"

"People spend their whole lives chasing. Careers. Houses. The right title, the right car, the right relationship. They think if they just get one more thing, they'll finally arrive."

"And they don't?"

"Some do. For a while."

He took a sip. Set the glass down.

"But most of them wake up old and realize they were so busy becoming someone that they forgot to be anyone."

The train swayed. Ice shifted in his glass.

"After Eleanor died, people kept telling me I'd find someone else. That I shouldn't be alone." He shook his head slowly. "But Eleanor was never what made me whole. That's not why I loved her. I loved her because we were both already whole. We chose each other. Every day, for thirty-seven years, we chose each other."

He was quiet for a moment. "Everyone gets it backwards."

"Gets what backwards?"

Richard looked at her. In the dim light, with the mountains behind him and the train moving beneath them and all the noise of the last few days finally gone quiet, he looked like what he was. A man near the end of something, trying to say something true.

"The biggest love affair of your life should be with yourself. With this life. With living it."

The words settled into the silence.

Part of her wanted to resist. It sounded like something you'd find on a bookmark in a gift shop, or cross-stitched on a pillow. The kind of wisdom that was easy to say and impossible to do.

But Richard wasn't selling anything. He was just sitting in an observation car at two in the morning, telling her what he'd figured out too late.

"Not selfish," he continued. "Not self-indulgence dressed up in better language. I mean actually knowing yourself. What makes you feel alive. What you're curious about. What terrifies you and thrills you and makes you feel like you're actually here. Present. Participating."

"I bought things," she said quietly. "For years. Things for the person I wanted to become. A yoga mat still in plastic. Italian flashcards I never got past 'grazie.' A pasta maker that's never seen pasta." She pulled the robe tighter. "I kept them in a closet. Like promises of someone I was planning to be."

"But you're here."

"I'm here."

Richard didn't say anything else. He didn't need to. The train kept moving, and outside the mountains kept passing, and she sat with the strange weight of it — thirty years of things she'd never used, and then one thing she had.

Maybe that was the whole difference. Between buying and using. Between someday and now.

They sat with that for a while. The train rocked gently. The mountains kept passing, patient and enormous and unconcerned.

"The foundation," Iris said finally. "You said it was part of what comes after."

"My entire estate. Medical research. Early detection. The things that might have saved Eleanor." He said it calmly, like he was discussing the weather. "Danny's been helping me arrange it all. He believes in it as much as I do."

"That's generous. Giving everything away."

"It's practical. I can't take it with me. And I'd rather it become something useful than sit in accounts while lawyers argue." He paused. "The lawyers have everything ready. I sign the final documents when we reach Istanbul."

He finished his drink. "It's not giving it away, really. It's turning it into something. Something that matters."

The sky outside was still dark, but different now. Softer at the edges. Not dawn yet, but the idea of it.

"I should let you rest," Iris said. "If you can."

"I'll sleep when I'm dead."

He caught her wince.

"Sorry. Danny hates that joke too."

She stood. At the door, she turned back.

"Richard. For what it's worth. I'm glad you're on this train."

"For what it's worth," he said, "I'm glad you spent your savings."

The corridor was still quiet. Still dimmed. She walked back to her cabin slowly, one hand on the wall, feeling the train move beneath her.

Fifty years old. And for the first time in longer than she could remember, she was curious about what came next.

Not anxious. Not braced. Just curious.

That felt new.

Her cabin door opened quietly. She turned on the small lamp by the desk. Found her journal. Opened to a fresh page.

For a moment she just sat there, pen hovering. Then she wrote:

The biggest love affair of your life should be with yourself. With this life. With living it.

Richard's words, in her handwriting now. Hers to keep.

She looked at the sentence. Felt slightly ridiculous.

She didn't cross it out.

Outside her window, the mountains were silver with moonlight. The train kept moving. Istanbul somewhere ahead, getting closer with every passing mile.

She closed the journal. Set down the pen.

Sleep still felt far away.

For once, she could live with that.

19

The lounge car that afternoon was full of people pretending to relax. Iris recognized the performance. She had done it herself often enough. Bodies arranged in comfortable positions, books held at the right angle, faces composed into expressions of leisure. But no one was actually reading. No one was actually calm. They were all just waiting for the next thing to happen and hoping it wouldn't.

Iris had claimed a chair in the corner with the Wharton she still hadn't managed to finish. Newland Archer was about to make a terrible decision. He'd been about to make it for forty pages now. She kept reading the same paragraph, waiting for him to do it, not quite able to care.

The elderly couple from car three had taken the settee nearest the window. They sat the way couples sat after fifty years of marriage. Close but not touching, each absorbed in their own activity, occasionally murmuring something the other didn't need to respond to. He had a newspaper. She had knitting. Neither seemed to be making progress. Every few minutes he'd turn a page he couldn't possibly have finished, and she'd count her stitches and frown and count them again.

Outside the windows, the Alps had finally decided to show themselves. After days of fog and murder and sitting still, the train was moving and the sky was clear and the mountains were doing that thing mountains did—looking permanent and ancient, as if nothing that happened in this train would even register. Iris found this oddly comforting. The Orient Express had seen a hundred years of scandals. The Alps had seen a hundred million. Perspective was useful.

Mrs. Winslow had claimed the largest settee and was doing what Mrs. Winslow did best: talking. The elderly couple had made the mistake of commenting on the view, and now they were trapped, nodding politely while she explained the principles of alpine horticulture.

"—of course, the borders are everything. Herbert always said a garden without structure was just weeds with ambition—"

Herbert. Everything circled back to Herbert. Herbert's theories on soil. Herbert's opinions on pruning. Herbert's firm beliefs about the proper height of delphiniums, which apparently was a thing one could have firm beliefs about.

The elderly woman's knitting needles clicked steadily. Her husband turned another page of his newspaper.

Iris turned a page she hadn't read.

"—and of course you have to plan in autumn if you want spring color. That's the secret nobody tells you. By the time you're thinking about gardens, it's already too late to have one—"

There was something soothing about Mrs. Winslow's voice, Iris decided. Not the content—she couldn't care less about perennial borders—but the rhythm of it. The steady stream of certainty. Mrs. Winslow knew exactly what she thought about gardens and husbands and the proper way to arrange a foyer, and she was going to share all of it whether you wanted her to or not.

It was restful, in its way. Like listening to a radio in another room.

"—and the soil, of course. People never think about soil. They think you just dig a hole and put a plant in it and hope for the best. But Herbert always said soil was everything. You wouldn't build a house on a bad foundation, would you? Same principle—"

Iris let the words wash over her. The train rocked gently. The mountains scrolled past. Newland Archer continued to teeter on the edge of his terrible decision.

She wondered what Robin was doing right now. Probably in the greenhouse, talking to her seedlings. Robin talked to plants the way other people talked to pets. Running commentary, gentle encouragement, occasional stern warnings about root rot. Iris had always found it charming. Now she found herself missing it with an intensity that surprised her.

She should have called Robin last night, after the conversation with Richard. Should have told her about the foundation, the confession, the strange intimacy of sitting in the dark with a dying man.

The biggest love affair of your life should be with yourself.

She'd written it down. It felt important. It still felt important.

"—the height in the back, of course, then you fill around it. Texture and color and form, all working together. Herbert used to say the right arrangement makes all the difference—"

The word landed.

She'd heard it before. Mrs. Winslow had used it days ago, and something had snagged then too. But Iris had been too overwhelmed to follow the thread. The investigation. Senn's questions. Her own name on a suspect list.

Now the thread pulled taut.

Like a lock turning. Like the moment when you'd been staring at something for hours and suddenly saw what had been there all along.

Arrangement.

Not a scheme. Not a con. Not Theo and Victoria plotting in corridors.

A flower arrangement.

The flowers in her cabin. The ones meant for Richard Hartwell, delivered to the wrong room. Danny in the corridor at 2:45 a.m.—*here you are*—helping Elena with something. She'd assumed glasses. But what if it was flowers? What if he was getting rid of them?

And the champagne toast. Danny at the tray with his surgeon's hands. Danny placing Richard's glass. Victoria grabbing the nearest one in a fury—

Richard's glass.

Iris's hands went cold.

She didn't have proof. She had a feeling—the kind of feeling that woke you at 3am, certain you'd left the stove on. The kind you couldn't explain but couldn't ignore.

She needed to know what those flowers were.

What had they looked like?

She closed her eyes. Tried to reach back through everything that had happened. The murder, the investigation, the handkerchief, Senn's questions, Theo's arrest. Layer after layer of crisis, burying that first day under an avalanche of everything that came after.

The platform at Victoria Station. The porter with her luggage. The corridor that smelled like furniture polish and money. Her hand on the brass door handle, not quite believing she was allowed to open it.

And then—the room.

She'd stood in the doorway like an idiot, just looking. The velvet. The wood paneling. The crystal fixtures throwing tiny rainbows across the ceiling. She'd felt like a minor character who'd wandered into the wrong story, like someone was going to tap her on the shoulder any moment and explain there'd been a mistake.

The marble bathroom had made her laugh out loud. Actual marble. On a train. She'd said something to herself about it, something about marble that traveled, marble with something to prove.

And on the writing desk—

The vase. Porcelain. Blue and white. Flowers spilling out of it like a welcome.

She tried to see them. Really see them, the way she'd seen them that afternoon before everything went wrong.

White roses. She remembered those clearly. Full and open and expensive-looking. The kind that probably cost more per stem than she spent on groceries in a week.

Dahlias. She was less certain about those, but something round and layered, coral-pink, filling the spaces between the roses.

And something else. Something smaller. Tucked in among the larger blooms like an afterthought.

Tiny white bells. Delicate. Clustered on thin green stems. She'd noticed them because they were pretty and because she didn't know what they were. Had thought about looking them up. Hadn't, because there was too much else to look at, too much else to feel, too many ways to be overwhelmed by the fact of being there at all.

She opened her eyes.

Mrs. Winslow was still talking. "—and the cutting garden, of course, is separate from the display garden. You can't mix utility with beauty, Herbert always said. One is for looking, one is for using. Different purposes, different spaces—"

The elderly woman had given up on her knitting. Her husband had given up on his newspaper. But Mrs. Winslow continued, oblivious, cheerfully explaining Herbert's philosophy of garden sheds.

Iris pulled out her phone.

The screen glowed. No signal. Still no signal. She typed a text anyway, to Robin, who would know. Robin with her greenhouse, her encyclopedic knowledge of anything that grew.

White flowers. Tiny bells on thin stems. What are they? Important.

The message sat there, unsent. Waiting for a signal that wasn't coming.

She stared at the screen. The little exclamation mark. Message not delivered.

Of course not. Of course the one time she actually needed to reach someone, the mountains were eating every signal that tried to escape.

Mrs. Winslow was fifteen feet away, talking about gardens.

Just ask her.

The thought sat there, obvious and terrifying.

Just ask. Confirm what you already know.

But what if she was wrong? What if the flowers were something ordinary, something harmless, something that had nothing to do with anything? She'd already helped get one man arrested based on a missing sketch. She'd already pointed Senn in a direction that had seemed so logical, so clear—

And Theo's face. That look of genuine surprise.

Iris looked at Mrs. Winslow. Looked at her phone. Looked at Mrs. Winslow again.

The elderly couple stood. Made their excuses. Mrs. Winslow looked momentarily bereft, a performer watching her audience leave.

Just ask. It's a question about flowers. People ask questions about flowers all the time. There's nothing suspicious about it.

Now. It had to be now.

"Mrs. Winslow."

The words came out too loud. Mrs. Winslow paused mid-sentence, eyebrows raised.

"Yes, dear?"

"I have a question. About flowers."

She heard her own voice—strained, strange. She made herself smile. It felt like wearing someone else's face. "There was an arrangement I saw. Earlier in the trip. I've been trying to figure out what one of the flowers was."

Mrs. Winslow's expression transformed. Delight. Pure, uncomplicated delight.

"Oh, how wonderful! I do love a botanical puzzle. What did they look like?"

"White roses," she said. "Dahlias, I think. And these tiny white flowers. Bell-shaped. Clustered together on stems."

"Bell-shaped," Mrs. Winslow repeated, considering. She tilted her head, the way a bird does when it's examining something interesting. "Clustered, you say? Like little lanterns?"

"Yes. Exactly."

"And the size? This matters, you know. People always forget to mention size. Were they large bells or small ones?"

"Small." Iris tried to remember. The vase on the desk. The afternoon light through the window. "Smaller than my fingernail. Delicate."

"Mm. And the stems, were they arching, or upright?"

"I—" She hadn't paid that much attention. She'd barely looked at them before the porter came back, apologizing, explaining they'd been delivered to the wrong cabin. "Arching, I think? They seemed to curve."

"Color of the stems?"

"Green. Just... green."

Mrs. Winslow nodded slowly, the way doctors nod when they're about to deliver a diagnosis.

"And the leaves? Did you notice the leaves, dear? That's often the key. Herbert always said you could identify any plant by its leaves if you knew what to look for."

"I—no. I don't think so. I didn't really look at the leaves."

"Pity. But never mind." Mrs. Winslow smiled, settling into her expertise.

"Based on what you've described—small white bells, clustered, arching stems—it sounds very much like lily of the valley. *Convallaria majalis.*"

She pronounced the Latin with evident pleasure, the way some people pronounced wine vintages.

"One of my absolute favorites. Herbert and I grew them along the north border for years. Thirty years of lily of the valley, can you imagine? They spread, of course. You have to contain them or they'll take over the whole garden. But such a lovely problem to have."

Lily of the valley. The name meant something. She was sure it meant something. But her mind had gone blank, all her half-remembered knowledge of flowers and gardens deserting her when she needed it most.

"They prefer shade," Mrs. Winslow continued, delighted to have a captive audience. "Most people don't realize that. They see them in bridal bouquets and assume they need sun, but actually the opposite is true. Too much sun and they wilt."

"Are they—" Iris stopped. Started again. Her voice sounded strange in her own ears. "What are they like? As a plant, I mean."

"Oh, quite lovely. That wonderful scent—sweet, fresh, almost intoxicating." Mrs. Winslow smiled. "They're quite hardy once established. Come back every year without any help. Herbert used to say they were the perfect flower for lazy gardeners." She laughed. "Not that he was ever lazy about anything."

"Mrs. Winslow." Iris heard the edge in her own voice. Tried to soften it. "Would they be safe? If someone had them in their home?"

"Safe?"

"I have a cat. At home. And I was thinking about maybe growing some. But I'd heard that certain flowers can be—"

"Oh, goodness no." Mrs. Winslow shook her head firmly. "You'd never grow lily of the valley if you had cats. Or dogs. Or small children, for that matter."

Iris's hands went cold.

"Why not?"

"They're poisonous, dear. Terribly poisonous. Every part of the plant—the leaves, the stems, the flowers, the roots. Even the water in the vase after they've been sitting for a day or two." She shook her head, still smiling, the way people did when discussing dangers that would never touch them. "Herbert used to joke they were nature's reminder that beauty could kill. Such a gorgeous plant, and every inch of it deadly."

The room was doing something strange. Tilting, maybe. Or holding too still. The velvet settees, the brass fixtures, the mountains outside the window—all of it suddenly felt very far away.

"What kind of poison?" Her voice came from somewhere outside herself.

"Cardiac glycosides, I believe. Similar to digitalis." Mrs. Winslow tilted her head, studying Iris with sudden attention. "Are you all right, dear? You've gone quite pale."

"What does that mean?" The words scraped out. "Cardiac glycosides?"

"Oh, it's all very technical. Something to do with the heart. The plant affects heart rhythms—makes them irregular, I think. Speeds them up or slows them down, I can never remember which." Mrs. Winslow waved a hand vaguely. "In tiny amounts it can actually be medicinal—that's where some heart medications come from, you know. But in larger doses..."

She made a tutting sound. The kind of sound you made about

the weather, or traffic, or anything that was unfortunate but not your problem.

"Very dangerous. Especially for anyone whose heart is already weak. An older person, or someone with a heart condition—it could be fatal quite quickly, I'd imagine."

Especially for anyone whose heart is already weak.

Richard's heart. Richard's failing heart. Richard who took pills every morning and every night, who touched his chest sometimes when he thought no one was watching. Richard who had told her last night that he was dying, that his heart was giving out, that the doctors had given him months.

Same thing that took Eleanor.

The flowers had been meant for his cabin. Not hers. The porter had apologized. Had moved them.

And then Danny had removed them. At a quarter to three in the morning. While everyone else was fighting and screaming.

Here you are.

Thank you, Mr. Morrison.

Not glasses. Not champagne flutes. Flowers. Evidence. Danny getting rid of the arrangement before anyone could connect it to anything.

We need to discuss the arrangement.

She'd thought it was Theo. Had filed it in the mental folder marked "suspicious behavior, night of murder" alongside the slammed doors and the screaming and Edmund's pathetic pounding on Victoria's door. The word had seemed to fit. Arrangement. Scheme. Con. The vocabulary of people up to something.

But Theo hadn't said arrangement. Someone else had been in that corridor at 4 a.m., and she'd assumed—

The champagne toast. The reconstruction. Danny at the tray, handling glasses with those surgeon's hands. Danny placing a flute in front of Richard.

Victoria, furious after Edmund's poem, storming away from their confrontation. Reaching for the nearest glass. Not her glass. Just the one closest to her.

Richard's glass.

The one Danny had placed there.

Oh god.

"—dear? Are you quite all right? You look like you might faint. Should I call someone? There's a doctor on board, I believe, a young man, very attentive—"

A doctor. She was talking about Danny. Of course she was talking about Danny.

"Fine." The word scraped out of her throat. "Just—the train. Motion sickness. I need some air."

She was standing. She didn't remember deciding to stand. The Wharton fell from her lap—she heard it hit the floor but didn't pick it up. Edith Wharton, spine up on the carpet of the Orient Express, and she was leaving it there because the floor was tilting and she had to get out of this room.

"Do you need assistance? Should I call someone?"

"No." Too sharp. She tried again. "No. Thank you. I'm fine. I just need—"

She didn't finish. She was already moving. Across the lounge car, past Mrs. Winslow's concerned face, past the settee the elderly couple had abandoned.

The door to the corridor. Her hand on the brass handle. Cold metal under her palm.

She pushed through.

The corridor was quiet. Dim. The afternoon light came through windows at intervals, throwing rectangles of gold onto the carpet. The train swayed gently. Her hand found the wall, and she leaned against it, breathing.

Think. Think.

The poison hadn't been in Victoria's champagne. It had been

in Richard's. Victoria had died because she'd grabbed the wrong glass at the wrong moment, reaching for the nearest one in her fury at Edmund.

It wasn't meant for her.

Richard was the target.

And Danny—

Danny who hovered. Danny who worried. Danny who was always there, at every meal, every conversation, helping Richard in and out of chairs, pouring his tea, watching him with those attentive eyes.

Danny who was a surgeon. Who knew about poisons. Who knew about hearts.

Danny who stood to inherit everything.

Except he wouldn't. Richard had told her that, last night in the observation car. The foundation. The will. Everything going to medical research. Danny had been helping arrange it all.

Danny knew.

Danny knew he was being cut out. Had known for months, maybe longer, while he smiled and poured tea and played the devoted nephew. And Richard — trusting, grateful Richard — had no idea that the man helping him build his legacy was planning to make sure it never happened.

I sign the final documents when we reach Istanbul.

If Richard died before Istanbul, those documents were worthless. The old will would stand. And Danny would inherit everything.

He wasn't racing against Richard's illness. He was racing against Richard's signature.

And Danny had already tried to kill Richard once. Had put lily of the valley in his cabin, had handled the champagne glasses, had set everything up perfectly—

Except Victoria had grabbed the wrong glass.

Iris's legs were shaking. She realized she was sliding down the wall and made herself stop. Made herself stand straight. The corridor stretched in both directions, velvet and brass and century-old wood, and somewhere on this train Danny was sitting with Richard, being the devoted nephew, biding his time.

The murderer is still on this train.

Theo had tried to tell her. Right there in the corridor, handcuffs on his wrists, officers pulling him away. He'd looked at her and tried to tell her.

The sketchbook. You told him about the sketchbook.

Iris pushed off from the wall. Her legs were steadier now. Still shaking, but functional. She could walk. She had to walk.

You have to warn Richard.

The thought crystallized. Clear and sharp and terrifying.

Richard didn't know. Richard thought Danny was his devoted nephew, his helper, his comfort in dying. Richard was going to sit with him at dinner tonight and have no idea that the man pouring his wine had already tried to kill him once.

She had to tell him. Had to find him alone, away from Danny, and tell him everything.

But Danny was always there. Every meal. Every conversation. Hovering. Watching. The devoted nephew who never left his uncle's side.

How was she supposed to get Richard alone when Danny never left?

Iris started walking. One foot in front of the other. The corridor swaying gently with the motion of the train.

She didn't know what she was going to do. Didn't have a plan. Just knew that she couldn't stand still, couldn't stay in one place, couldn't let this knowledge sit inside her without doing something.

The last thought was the worst. The one that kept circling back, landing in her chest like a stone.

She'd noticed what nobody else noticed. She'd pointed Senn

toward Theo. She'd given Danny exactly what he needed—a scapegoat, an arrest, a closed case.

Thirty years of helping people find the right answers, and she'd handed Senn the wrong one. If Theo rotted in prison, it would be partly her fault.

If Richard died, it would be partly her fault.

She'd been so proud of herself. So pleased to have solved the puzzle. The librarian who noticed things, who saw what others missed. And all along she'd been seeing exactly what Danny wanted her to see.

The corridor ended. Another car. More velvet, more brass, more impossibly soft carpet.

Somewhere on this train, Danny was waiting.

And she was the only one who knew.

20

Iris kept one hand on the wall and kept walking. Her legs felt strange beneath her — not quite her own, not quite reliable. Away from the lounge car. Away from Mrs. Winslow's cheerful voice still explaining something about Herbert and shade gardens.

A door opened ahead of her. Margaret emerged, disapproval already forming on her face at the sight of someone moving too quickly through the corridor.

"Are you quite—"

"Fine," Iris said. "I'm fine. Excuse me."

She pushed past without stopping. Margaret said something sharp behind her, but the words didn't land. Iris was already turning the corner, already through the connecting door, already counting the cabin numbers as she passed them. Seven. Eight. Nine. Counting was something to do. Counting kept the panic at a manageable distance.

Her phone was in her hand. She didn't remember taking it out.

No signal. Of course no signal. But she held it up anyway,

watching the empty bars, willing them to appear. Moved to the window. Held it higher. As if the extra six inches would make any difference.

Nothing.

She typed a text anyway, thumbs clumsy on the screen.

Robin. Emergency. Danny Morrison killed Victoria. Poison—lily of the valley. Richard was the target. I'm trapped on this train with him. Please call someone.

Sending. Sending. Failed to send.

She tried again. Because trying felt better than standing still and she needed something to do with her hands besides shake.

The red exclamation marks stared back at her. Not delivered. Not delivered. Not delivered.

Robin's voice in her head: *That's not how cell towers work, Iris.*

Fair point.

For a brief, absurd second, she thought about texting Janet. Janet from the library. Janet who had once called Iris at 11 p.m. to ask whether "inflammable" and "flammable" meant the same thing, because she was writing a letter to her landlord and wanted to be precise. Janet who had spent three weeks convinced the new copier was sentencing, because it kept printing her documents in the wrong order. Janet who would receive a text saying *I'm trapped on a train with a murderer* and somehow conclude that Iris needed help finding a book about trains.

She would also try very hard to be helpful. Janet always *tried.*

Iris put the phone back in her pocket.

She needed to think. The corridor offered nothing — just brass and carpet and closed doors and the faint smell of furniture polish. No answers. No allies. Just her, and everything she now knew, and the fact that she couldn't unknow it.

Richard.

The thought surfaced like a gasp. Richard, three cars away.

Richard, who might be napping peacefully in his cabin. Or Richard, who might be accepting a cup of tea from Danny right now, the way he'd accepted a hundred cups of tea, never once suspecting that the hands preparing it had already tried to kill him once.

She thought about the champagne glass. Danny's surgeon hands at the tray. Victoria grabbing the nearest flute in her fury — not her glass, Richard's glass. A death meant for someone else, delivered to the wrong person by pure bad luck.

Danny wouldn't make that mistake twice. Next time, he'd be sure.

If there is a next time. If there hasn't already been.

The thought propelled her forward before she could talk herself out of it.

Richard's cabin was three doors down. She knocked, felt her pulse jump into her throat, and immediately wished she hadn't. What was she going to say? *I think your nephew is trying to kill you?* Richard would think she'd lost her mind. Richard trusted Danny completely. Richard had spent their entire midnight conversation talking about how Danny had helped him build the foundation, how Danny understood, how Danny was the one person he could count on.

How did you tell someone that the person they loved most was the person they should fear?

Footsteps inside.

The door opened.

Danny.

Iris felt her stomach lurch sideways. Her hand tightened on the doorframe — she hadn't realized she'd been gripping it — and she made herself loosen her fingers before he noticed. Before he saw. Before he understood that she understood.

Smile. Say something normal. Don't let him see.

"Iris." Danny smiled. The one that had made her feel included, welcomed, and like she had belonged at their table. "What a nice surprise."

She watched his face for any sign that he knew. Any crack in the pleasantness. But Danny had always been seamless, hadn't he? She'd admired that about him once. She'd thought it was kindness.

Now she wondered if it was practice.

"I was hoping to speak with Richard." She heard her own voice — too bright, too strained, the voice of someone trying very hard to sound casual. "Is he in?"

"He's resting, actually. The excitement of the past few days caught up with him." Danny leaned against the doorframe, his body blocking the gap, casual and immovable. "Is it urgent? I can wake him if—"

"No. No, don't wake him." She made herself smile back. It felt like holding a book open to the wrong page. "It can wait. I just wanted to... check on him."

"That's kind of you. I'll let him know you stopped by."

"Thank you."

She should leave. She knew she should leave. But her feet wouldn't move, and Danny's eyes were on her face—reading her the way he'd read a chart. Looking for what was wrong.

"Are you all right?" he asked. His voice softened with concern. "You seem... upset."

"Fine. Just tired. Like everyone."

"Of course." He nodded slowly. "It's been a difficult week."

"Yes. It has."

She made herself turn. Made herself walk away. She could feel him still standing there—that prickle between the shoulder blades she'd learned to recognize after decades of patrons waiting for her to look up. She didn't look back.

He knows something's wrong.

Maybe not what. But something. She'd stood there too long. Asked too few questions. Smiled with too much effort.

She turned the corner and stopped, pressing her back against the wall. Her heart was pounding. Her hands were shaking. She'd just stood three feet from a murderer and pretended everything was fine, and she had no idea if she'd been convincing.

Think. Think.

She couldn't get to Richard — not with Danny standing guard. She couldn't call anyone — not with the mountains swallowing every signal. She couldn't go to Senn. Senn was gone, and he'd arrested the wrong man anyway.

What did that leave?

The conductor. The train had to have some way of communicating with the outside world. A radio. A satellite phone. Something for emergencies. If she could reach the conductor, explain what she'd learned—

He'd think she was crazy. A passenger spinning theories about poison flowers and champagne glasses. He'd smile politely and suggest she rest.

Unless she had proof. Unless she had someone who could confirm at least part of the story.

Elena.

Elena had been in that corridor at a quarter to three in the morning. Elena had taken the flowers from Danny. *Here you are. Thank you, Mr. Morrison.* Iris had assumed glasses at the time. But it could have been flowers. It could have been Danny handing off the evidence, disposing of the arrangement before anyone could connect it to anything.

If Elena remembered. If Elena would talk to her. If Elena would tell someone who mattered.

It wasn't much. But it was something.

The conductor's office first. Then Elena.

Iris pushed off from the wall and started walking.

THE CONDUCTOR'S OFFICE WAS NEAR THE FRONT OF THE TRAIN, PAST THE dining car and through two connecting doors. She'd passed it once before, on her second day aboard — a small door with a brass plate reading STAFF ONLY, always closed, always unremarkable. She hadn't given it a second thought at the time. It was just part of the scenery. Part of the machinery that kept everything running while passengers ate and drank and pretended they were in a novel.

She found it now. Knocked.

No answer.

She knocked again, harder. The brass plate rattled slightly.

"Hello? Is anyone—"

A steward appeared from the next car — not Elena, but a young man she'd seen once or twice, refilling water glasses at dinner. He had the alert, slightly nervous look of someone new to the job and determined not to make mistakes.

"Can I help you, madam?"

"I need to speak with the conductor. It's urgent."

"I'm afraid he's occupied at the moment. Is there something I can assist with?"

Yes. There's a murderer on this train. The wrong man was arrested. The real killer is sitting three cars away, probably planning how to finish what he started. I need someone with a radio and authority and the ability to do something about it.

She couldn't say any of that. She'd sound unhinged. The steward would smile politely and file her away as "difficult passenger, cabin 7."

"When will he be available?"

"I'm not certain, madam. Perhaps after dinner service?" His expression was apologetic but firm. The face of someone trained to say no while making it sound like concern. "If you'd like to leave a message, I can make sure he receives it."

"No. Thank you."

She walked away. The steward's eyes followed her — she could feel them — and she kept her pace steady, her posture normal. Nothing to see here. Just a woman who'd wanted to speak to the conductor about something trivial. Seating arrangements, maybe. A complaint about the water pressure.

Elena.

Elena was her only option now. Elena, who had taken the flowers. Elena, who might remember what Danny had said, what time it had been, how he'd explained the request. Elena, who could at least confirm that the arrangement had existed. That it had been removed. That Danny had been the one to ask.

It wasn't proof of murder. But it was a thread. A piece of the story that didn't depend on Iris's word alone.

THE SERVICE AREA WAS TUCKED BETWEEN CARS — A NARROW CORRIDOR lined with storage compartments and small doors marked with numbers and abbreviations Iris didn't understand. It smelled faintly of coffee and something citrusy, the kind of industrial cleaner that tried to smell pleasant and didn't quite manage it.

Elena was there, alone, standing at a small counter making notes on a clipboard. A stack of linens sat beside her, waiting to be sorted. A coffee cup with a chipped handle. The practical clutter of someone else's work, someone else's world.

The rest of the train had gone quiet. Iris could feel it — that particular stillness of early evening, when most passengers had retreated to their cabins to rest before dinner. The Ashfords were probably behind their closed door, not speaking. Edmund was probably drinking alone somewhere, rehearsing his grievances. Mrs. Winslow had probably exhausted her audience and moved on to a nap. Even the stewards had grown sparse, visible only in glimpses at the ends of corridors.

It was the kind of quiet that should have felt peaceful. Instead, it felt like everyone was holding their breath.

Elena looked up, surprise crossing her face. "Ms. Quinn. Is everything all right?"

Iris glanced up and down the corridor. Empty. Just the two of them.

"Elena." She kept her voice low. "I need to ask you something. It's important."

"Of course." Elena set down the clipboard. Her posture shifted — not unfriendly, but careful. The posture of someone whose job required navigating difficult conversations. "What can I help you with?"

"The night of the murder. You were working. Collecting glasses, cleaning up after everything that happened."

Elena nodded slowly. Something guarded moved behind her eyes.

"Someone helped you. In the corridor. Around a quarter to three in the morning." Iris watched Elena's face, looking for recognition. "They handed you something. Do you remember?"

Elena's frown deepened. "I'm not sure what you—"

"Flowers. An arrangement. From Mr. Hartwell's cabin." Iris kept her voice steady, though her heart was pounding so hard she was certain Elena could hear it. "Someone asked you to get rid of them."

For a moment, Elena's face stayed blank. Polite confusion. The expression of someone trying to help but not understanding the question.

Iris felt her stomach sink. *She doesn't remember. It was the middle of the night, the whole train was chaos, she probably moved a dozen things from a dozen places—*

Then something shifted. A small change in Elena's expression. Recognition, surfacing slowly.

"There was an arrangement," Elena said. Her voice was careful, measuring each word. "Mr. Morrison asked me to remove it. He said Mr. Hartwell was having trouble sleeping, that the scent was bothering him."

"Mr. Morrison." Iris's mouth was dry. "Danny Morrison."

"He stopped me in the corridor. Said the arrangement in Mr. Hartwell's cabin was giving him headaches, could I remove it and dispose of it." Elena paused, her brow furrowing. "Is something wrong?"

The pieces slid together with a quiet, horrible neatness. Not a theory anymore. Not a hunch. A straight line from point to point: an arrangement ordered, an arrangement removed, a glass of champagne, a death.

"Elena," Iris said. She leaned in despite herself, lowering her voice further. "Those flowers were poisonous. Lily of the valley. They're deadly to someone with a weak heart. Richard Hartwell has a failing heart."

Elena's face went pale.

"The champagne that killed Victoria — I think it was meant for Richard. The glass Danny placed in front of him. Victoria grabbed the wrong one." Iris stopped. Started again. The words felt too big for this small space between storage compartments and linens. "I need to reach the conductor. Or the police. Someone with authority. Is there a way to send a message from the train? A radio, or—"

Elena's eyes moved past her.

Just for a second. A tiny shift of attention, there and gone.

Iris felt her stomach drop. The corridor behind her, which had been empty a moment ago. The silence, which had been ordinary, now felt like something else entirely.

She turned.

Danny was standing at the end of the corridor.

Not moving. Not speaking. Just standing there, hands loose at his sides, watching them with an expression of mild curiosity. The devoted nephew, out for an evening stroll. Looking for something. Looking for someone.

Looking for her.

How long has he been there?

The question screamed through her mind. Had he heard his name? Had he heard *lily of the valley*? Had he heard *the champagne was meant for Richard*? She tried to replay the last thirty seconds, tried to remember how loud her voice had been, whether the words had carried. But she couldn't be sure. She couldn't be sure of anything except that he was here now, and Elena had seen him, and the corridor suddenly felt very small and very long.

"There you are, Iris." Danny started toward them. Unhurried. Pleasant. "I was looking for you. Richard woke up, and I mentioned you'd stopped by. He was hoping to see you."

"That's... that's good," Iris said. Her voice sounded strange in her own ears. Too thin. Too careful. "I'll come by later."

"Actually, I thought we might have tea first." He stopped beside her, close enough that she could smell his cologne — something expensive and subtle, the kind of scent that didn't announce itself. "You seemed upset earlier. I wanted to make sure you were all right."

His hand found her elbow. Light and polite. The same way he'd touched Richard a hundred times, guiding him into chairs, helping him up stairs. Careful. Solicitous. Impossible to refuse without making a scene.

"Elena," Danny said, turning to her with that same warm smile, "would you bring us a tea service? We'll be in the observation car."

"Of course, Mr. Morrison." Elena's voice stayed carefully neutral. Her face gave nothing away. But her eyes met Iris's for a single moment — loaded, uncertain — and then she was gathering her clipboard and retreating down the corridor, disappearing through a door marked STAFF.

Iris watched her go. The last person who knew. The last person who might be able to do something. Walking away, because what else could she do? Danny was a guest. Iris was a guest. Elena was an employee on a train that paid her salary.

"Come on," Danny said. His hand stayed on her arm — not gripping, not hurting, just *there*. Present. Inescapable. "Let's sit somewhere comfortable."

He smiled. The same smile he'd given her at tea that first day, when he'd taught her about brewing temperatures and offered her honey from a farm in the Cotswolds.

"I think we should talk."

21

The observation car was empty.

Late afternoon light poured through the windows, turning everything amber and gold. The same velvet chairs from three days ago. The same brass fixtures. The same view of the Alps, still magnificent, still indifferent. That was the thing about beautiful rooms. They just kept being beautiful, no matter what was about to happen in them.

Danny gestured to the chairs by the window.

Iris sat. Not because she wanted to—because Elena was coming. Elena, who had heard everything in the service corridor. Elena, who might do something, tell someone, find a way to help. Until that tea service arrived, the smartest thing Iris could do was not make him angry.

He took the seat across from her, settling into the same place he'd chosen that first afternoon, when tea had been just tea and she'd been charmed by a man who knew about brewing temperatures.

"So," Danny said. "Tell me what's wrong."

"Nothing's wrong."

"Iris." His voice was gentle. Patient. The voice of a man who had all the time in the world. "I've spent ten years reading patients. I know when someone's hiding something."

She didn't answer. Every response she could think of felt like a trap.

Danny studied her the way he'd studied her that first day. With attention. With focus. With the particular care of someone who wanted to understand.

"You've been acting strangely since this afternoon," he said. "Leaving the lounge so suddenly. Coming by Richard's cabin. Talking to Elena in the service corridor." A pause. "About flowers."

The train swayed. The mountains kept sliding past. Somewhere, a door opened and closed.

"I didn't hear everything," he continued. "But I heard enough to be concerned."

"Concerned about what?"

"About you." He leaned forward. "Iris, I think you've been under enormous stress. The murder. Being suspected. Theo's arrest. It's enough to make anyone start seeing patterns that aren't there."

"I'm not—"

"The flowers were bothering Richard. He gets headaches from strong scents—always has. I asked Elena to remove them. That's all." He spread his hands. Open. Reasonable. "That's the whole story."

He sounded so calm. So certain. So exactly like a man telling the truth.

Maybe he is, part of her whispered. *Maybe you're wrong. Maybe you've done it again—built a case out of coincidences, pointed at the wrong person, ruined another life.*

She thought about Theo. The handcuffs. The look of genuine surprise.

The murderer is still on this train.

The door opened.

Elena entered with the tea service. Silver tray, white porcelain, two cups. She crossed the car and set it down on the table between them.

Her eyes met Iris's for just a moment.

I heard you. I know.

But what could Elena do? She was staff. Danny was a guest. There were rules, hierarchies, the whole machinery of service that kept people in their places.

"Thank you, Elena," Danny said. "That will be all."

Elena hesitated. The smallest pause—a breath held half a second too long.

Then she turned and walked out. The door closed behind her with a soft click.

Danny reached into his jacket pocket and produced a small jar. Not the Cotswolds honey she remembered—something darker, more amber.

"I found a new honey," he said. "The porter sourced it from a monastery in the Engadin Valley. Benedictine monks, apparently. They've kept bees there for three hundred years."

He unscrewed the lid, inhaled appreciatively.

"The bees forage on alpine wildflowers. Edelweiss, gentian, wild orchid." He spooned some into one of the cups. "Lily of the valley grows in those meadows too. Gives it an unusual sweetness."

The name landed in the silence like a stone dropped into still water.

Iris kept her face neutral. Watched him watching her.

"The monks believe the honey has restorative properties," Danny continued. "Medieval superstition, of course. But there's something appealing about it. The idea that sweetness can heal."

He poured the tea. Set one cup in front of her.

She didn't touch it.

"You think I killed Victoria." Not a question. His voice was quiet. Sad, almost. "You think I poisoned a woman I'd never met."

"I think the champagne was meant for Richard."

Danny was quiet for a moment. When he spoke again, his voice had the careful gentleness of someone talking to a child who'd said something embarrassing.

"Iris. Richard is dying. His heart is failing. The doctors have given him months—a year at most." He picked up his own cup, cradled it in his hands. "Why would I need to hurry that along? Why would I risk everything—my career, my freedom, my relationship with the only family I have left—when all I had to do was wait?"

Because waiting gets you nothing.

The foundation. The signature in Istanbul. The deadline he couldn't let Richard reach.

She didn't say any of it. Just sat with her cold tea and let him think he'd won the point.

He took a sip of his tea. Unhurried. Calm.

She had no answer. Put that way, it sounded absurd. The paranoid fantasy of a woman who'd read too many mysteries.

"I've spent ten years taking care of him," Danny said. "After my parents died—car accident, I was nineteen—Richard was the one who showed up. Paid for medical school. Helped me build a practice. Called me every Sunday, even when I was too busy to call him back."

His voice caught slightly. The grief in it sounded real.

"He's the last family I have. And you think my response to losing him is *murder*."

Iris looked at her untouched tea. The steam rising from it. The honey already dissolved, invisible now.

"The flowers were poisonous," she said. "Lily of the valley. Every part of the plant is toxic."

"Lots of flowers are toxic. Foxglove. Oleander. Azaleas." Danny shrugged. "It doesn't mean everyone who buys a bouquet is planning a murder."

"You removed them. In the middle of the night."

"Because Richard couldn't sleep. The scent was bothering him." A flash of something—frustration, maybe—crossed his face. "I've removed hundreds of things from Richard's room over the years. Books that upset him. Food that disagreed with him. Flowers that gave him headaches. It's what I do. It's what I've always done."

He set down his cup. Leaned back.

"Drink your tea, Iris. It's getting cold."

She didn't move.

"I understand," he said. "After everything you've been through, it must be hard to trust anyone. But I'm not your enemy. I'm worried about you. We all are."

We.

"Richard's been asking about you," Danny continued. "He's grown very fond of you, you know. Said you reminded him of Eleanor. The way you listen. The way you notice things." A small smile. "He doesn't say that lightly."

His voice was steady. His face was composed. But his hand, when he reached for the teapot, had the slightest tremor.

The untouched cup sat between them. Getting cold.

"You haven't tried your tea," Danny said.

"I'm not thirsty."

"It's very good. The honey really does make a difference."

"You mentioned that."

"You should try it."

"No."

The word came out flatter than she intended. Final.

Danny was quiet. Looking at her. Looking at the cup she wasn't drinking.

"Iris." His voice was very soft now. "What do you think is in that cup?"

"Tea."

"Then why won't you drink it?"

"I told you. I'm not thirsty."

"You came from the lounge car. You walked through three cars to Richard's cabin, then to the conductor's office, then to the service area. You've been moving nonstop for an hour." He tilted his head. "And you're not thirsty."

She didn't answer.

"You think I poisoned it." Not a question. "You think I put something in the honey."

"I didn't say that."

"You didn't have to." He sat back. Studied her. "You know, I've been a doctor for fifteen years. I've had patients accuse me of all kinds of things. Mistakes I didn't make. Motives I didn't have. It comes with the job."

He picked up her cup. Held it.

"But I've never had someone look at me the way you're looking at me right now."

For a moment, she thought he was going to drink it. Prove her wrong. Make her feel foolish and paranoid and exactly as crazy as he'd been suggesting she was.

Instead, he set the cup down. Gently. Precisely. Exactly where it had been.

"The thing about accusations," he said, "is that they're very hard to take back. Once you've said something—once you've really said it—you can't unsay it. The words just sit there. Between people. Forever."

He leaned forward.

"So before you say anything else—to me, to Richard, to the conductor, to anyone—I want you to think very carefully about whether you're sure. Whether you're absolutely sure."

The light had shifted while they talked. The amber had deepened to bronze, the shadows stretching longer across the velvet. The mountains outside were going purple at their edges.

"Because if you're wrong," Danny continued, "you'll have destroyed the only family I have left. Richard's last months will be spent wondering whether his nephew—the person who gave up everything to take care of him—is a murderer." A pause. "And I will never forgive you for that."

His voice was calm. Reasonable. Almost kind.

And underneath it, cold and clear as glacier water: a threat.

"Well!"

The voice came from the doorway. Sharp, familiar, utterly unexpected.

Mrs. Winslow stood at the entrance to the observation car, slightly out of breath, a paperback clutched in one hand.

"I've been looking everywhere for this. Left it here after lunch and couldn't remember where I'd—" She stopped. Looked at them. The tableau they made—the untouched tea, the careful distance, the quality of silence.

"Am I interrupting something?"

"No," Danny said. "We were just finishing up."

"We were," Iris agreed. She stood. Her legs felt distant, not quite connected to the rest of her. "I was just leaving."

"Don't let me chase you off," Mrs. Winslow said, settling into a chair with the determination of a woman who had found her spot and intended to keep it. "I'll just be here with my book. Don't mind me."

Iris moved toward the door. Felt Danny's attention following her.

"Iris." His voice was pleasant. Easy. "Think about what I said."

"I will."

"And get some rest. You look exhausted."

She walked out of the car. Down the corridor. One foot in front of the other, the brass fixtures blurring past, the carpet swallowing her footsteps.

Think about what I said.

She was thinking. That was the problem. She couldn't stop.

Richard's door was three cars away. She walked faster. The train swayed and she swayed with it, one hand trailing along the wall, counting doors like she'd counted them an hour ago. Seven. Eight. Nine.

She knocked.

"Richard." Her voice came out strange, scraped thin. "Richard, please—"

The door opened.

Richard stood there, reading glasses pushed up on his forehead, a book in one hand. He looked tired. Older than he'd looked three days ago.

"Iris? What's wrong?"

She pushed past him into the cabin. Closed the door. Locked it.

"Iris, you're scaring me—"

"Danny," she said. The word came out breathless, ragged. "Danny killed Victoria. And I think he just tried to poison me."

Richard stared at her.

She was aware, distantly, that she looked insane. Standing in a locked cabin, hair escaping from whatever she'd done to it that morning, telling a man she'd known for three days that his beloved nephew was a murderer.

In books, this was the part where the detective laid out the evidence. Calm. Methodical. Convincing.

She had a teacup she hadn't drunk. A flower she couldn't prove. And the feeling—the absolute certainty in her bones—that she'd just escaped something terrible.

22

Richard was staring at her like she'd lost her mind.

Fair enough. She was breathless, shaking, wild-eyed. She probably looked like she'd lost her mind.

"Iris, what on earth—"

"I need to tell you something." She closed the door behind her. Leaned against it. Her lungs were burning. "It's about Danny."

Richard's expression shifted. Concern, but not the kind she needed. Concern for Danny, not for himself.

"What about Danny? Did something happen?"

"He's fine. Everyone is fine." She was babbling. She needed to stop babbling.

She pressed her hands to her face. Took a breath. "I'm going to tell you something, and you're not going to believe me. But I need you to listen. All of it. Before Danny comes back."

"Iris." Richard's voice was gentle. The same voice he'd used in the observation car, talking about Eleanor and Tuscany and all the things he'd never gotten around to doing. "You're shaking. Sit down. Tell me what's wrong."

She sat. The chair was too soft. The kind that swallowed you when you needed to stay alert. She perched on the edge, knees pressed together, hands gripping the armrests.

Richard lowered himself into the chair across from her. His reading glasses were still pushed up on his forehead, forgotten.

"The flowers," she said. "The arrangement in my cabin the first day. The one that was meant for your cabin."

Richard frowned. "The mix-up. Yes, I remember. The porter apologized—"

"Lily of the valley."

He waited. The name clearly meant nothing to him.

"It's a flower. White bells, very pretty, very traditional." She heard herself sounding like a reference librarian. *Here are the facts, sir. Here is what you need to know.*

"Also extremely poisonous. Every part of the plant. The flowers, the stems, even the water in the vase. Cardiac glycosides. The same compounds they use in heart medication. The same compounds that, in the wrong dose, will stop a heart entirely."

Richard was very still.

"Someone ordered an arrangement with those flowers for your cabin," Iris continued. "And then, the night of the murder, someone removed them. Around a quarter to three in the morning. I heard it through my wall. A voice in the corridor, talking to Elena. I assumed they were collecting glasses. Cleaning up after all the drama." She paused. "It wasn't glasses. It was the flowers. Someone was getting rid of them before anyone could connect them to anything."

"Iris—"

"The champagne toast. The reconstruction Senn made us do." She couldn't stop now. The words were pouring out, the things she'd been holding onto finally refusing to stay quiet. "Danny was at the tray. You remember? He was handling the glasses, picking them up, setting them down, very particular about which one went where. And then he brought glasses back to our table. Placed yours right in front of you."

Richard's hand moved to his chest. That gesture she'd noticed before, the unconscious tell of a man whose heart was always on his mind.

"Victoria was angry," Iris said. "After Edmund's poem. After she slapped him. She wanted champagne. She just grabbed the nearest glass. Didn't look, didn't think. Just grabbed."

"My glass." Richard's voice was barely audible.

"Yes."

Silence. The train rocked beneath them. Outside the window, the mountains slid past, catching the last of the afternoon light.

"You're saying Victoria was poisoned by accident," Richard said slowly. "That she drank something meant for me."

"Yes."

"And you're saying Danny—" He stopped. His jaw tightened. "You're saying my nephew, who has been with me for twenty years, who has taken care of me through every illness and surgery and scare, tried to kill me with poisoned flowers and champagne."

"Yes."

Richard stood up. Walked to the window. His back was to her, shoulders rigid.

"That's insane."

"I know how it sounds—"

"Do you?" He turned. His face had changed. The gentle philosopher from the observation car was gone, replaced by something harder. The man who'd built companies. The man who hadn't gotten rich by believing everything he was told. "You've known me for less than a week. You've known Danny for less than a week. And you're standing in my cabin telling me that the boy I raised, the only family I have left, is a murderer."

"There has to be another explanation." He was pacing now, three steps toward the window, three steps back. "The flowers...anyone could have ordered them. The train, the travel company, some service that sends arrangements to first-class passengers. And removing them at night. Danny's always doing things like that. Last month he threw out a candle I'd had for years because he said the scent was giving me headaches."

"Was it?"

"I—" Richard stopped pacing. "I don't remember."

"Based on what?" His voice was rising now. "Flowers? A glass at a party? You heard someone in a corridor and you've decided it was Danny?"

"The flowers were ordered for your cabin," Iris said. "They were delivered to mine by mistake. The porter moved them to you."

"By mistake. Yes, I remember."

"And then they were removed. In the middle of the night. Danny asked Elena to dispose of them."

Richard shook his head. "Maybe they wilted. Maybe someone complained about the smell. There are a dozen explanations that don't involve attempted murder."

Iris opened her mouth. Closed it. He was right—of course he was right. Every piece of evidence she had could be explained away. Coincidence. Misunderstanding. The imaginings of a woman who'd been through too much in the last few days and had read one too many mysteries.

But she knew. She knew the way you knew when a book was misshelved, when something was wrong in the stacks even if you couldn't say exactly what. The pattern was there.

She had one card left.

"The foundation," she said quietly.

Richard went still.

"You're giving away your estate. All of it. Medical research, early detection. The kind of work that might have saved Eleanor."

She watched his face. "Danny helped you set it up. He knows about it."

"He's been very supportive."

"He knows the money isn't coming to him. He's known for a while. And he helped you anyway. Smiled and nodded and played the supportive nephew while you planned to give away everything he thought was his."

"The papers aren't signed yet." Richard's voice was quiet now. "The foundation doesn't legally exist until Istanbul. Until then, the previous will—"

He stopped.

Something shifted in his face. Not disbelief anymore. Something worse.

"If I die before Istanbul," he said slowly, "the foundation doesn't happen. Everything reverts to the old will."

"And Danny knows exactly when those papers are scheduled to be signed."

The words hung there. The final piece, falling into place.

"The flowers," Richard said. His voice was barely a whisper. "You're sure it was lily of the valley?"

"Mrs. Winslow identified them. Said they're beautiful. Traditional. And deadly to anyone with heart problems."

Richard laughed. It was a terrible sound. Broken, hollow, the sound of something giving way inside.

"Danny's a cardiac surgeon," he said. "He's been managing my medications for two years. Every pill, every dosage. He knows exactly what my heart can handle." He paused. "And exactly what it can't."

Iris said nothing. There was nothing to say.

"The same knowledge that kept me alive." Richard's voice was barely audible. "He could have used it any time. Any time at all."

He was quiet for a long moment. Then he walked slowly to the bed and sat down on the edge, lowering himself carefully, like a man who had suddenly become aware of how breakable he was.

"He was twelve when his parents died," Richard said. His voice was different now. Softer. "Twelve years old, standing in my living room, trying not to cry because someone had told him that men don't cry. I promised him I'd take care of him. I promised his mother—my sister—that I'd make sure he was okay."

Iris said nothing.

"I paid for everything. College, medical school, residency. Watched him become one of the best cardiac surgeons in his field." Richard stared at the floor. "When Eleanor got sick, he was there. Every appointment. Every consultation. He read every study, talked to every specialist. When she died—" His voice cracked. "When she died, he sat with me for a week. Didn't try to fix it. Didn't try to make it better. Just sat."

Iris felt something shift in her chest. This wasn't what she'd expected. She'd expected denial, resistance, the defensive anger of a man protecting his family. She hadn't expected grief. She hadn't expected Richard to sit there on the edge of his bed, mourning a relationship that might never have been real.

She'd filed Danny under "devoted nephew" the same way she'd sorted everyone else on this train. But people weren't genres. They didn't always stay in their categories.

"I taught him to drive," Richard said. "Six Saturdays in an empty parking lot, letting him grind the clutch on my Mercedes." He looked up at her. "You're asking me to believe the boy who cried when he finally passed his test wanted me dead."

"I don't know what he wanted." Iris's voice came out smaller than she intended. "Maybe he did love you. Once. Maybe he still does, in some way. But people can love someone and still—"

"Still what? Still poison them?"

"Still want what they think they're owed."

The train rocked. The light outside was fading, the mountains going purple at their edges.

“No. He loves me," Richard said.

Iris didn't know what to say. Some losses didn't leave room for words.

She thought of Robin, who would have known exactly what to say. Robin always knew.

The door opened.

Danny stood in the doorway, just a little winded, as if he'd come after her more quickly than he meant to admit. By the time Iris looked up, his face had already rearranged itself into concern. That familiar, careful expression he wore whenever Richard needed him.

His eyes moved between them, quick and precise, not missing a thing.

"What's going on?"

Iris watched Richard's face. Watched him look at Danny. Watched him decide.

23

Nobody moved.

Danny stood in the doorway. *What's going on?* But he wasn't really asking. She could see it in the way his eyes moved. Richard on the bed. Iris too close. The particular quality of silence that only happened when people had been talking about you.

He'd known since the tea. Maybe before.

"She had a nightmare," Richard said. His voice was almost steady. "She was upset. Came to talk."

Danny stepped into the cabin and closed the door behind him.

The click of the latch was very loud.

"A nightmare." He wasn't looking at Richard. He was looking at Iris. "You were asking Elena about flowers. About an arrangement I removed. About me."

Iris said nothing. There was nothing to say that would help.

"And then you ran."

"Danny—" Richard started.

"Don't."

The word landed. Then whatever had slipped was back behind his eyes, smoothed over, pleasant again.

"Please. We're past that now."

The cabin felt smaller than it had a moment ago. Three people. Not enough air.

Through the window, the mountains were lower now. Buildings in the distance. Trackside lights flashing past. The world outside continuing as if nothing were happening in here.

"Tell me she's wrong," Richard said.

Danny looked at his uncle then. Really looked. Something moved across his face—not guilt, exactly. Something older.

"Would it matter if I did?"

"Yes." Richard's hand went to his chest. "It would matter."

The silence stretched.

"I rehearsed this," Danny said. "For months. What I'd say if it ever came out." He shook his head. "It all sounds ridiculous now."

Richard made a sound Iris had never heard from him before. Something between a gasp and a sob. He sank onto the edge of the bed. Slowly. Like a man whose strings had been cut.

She'd seen this before. At the library, sometimes. A phone call at the reference desk. A letter opened in the reading room. The moment when the world shifted and the person hadn't caught up yet.

The body always knew first.

"The night I decided," Danny said, "we had dinner in London. That Italian place Eleanor loved."

"Don't," Richard said. "Don't use her name."

Danny stopped. For a moment, something flickered—surprise, maybe. He wasn't used to Richard pushing back.

"You talked about the foundation for two hours," he continued, quieter now. "The research grants. The building you wanted to name after her. And then you said—'Danny, I'm so glad you understand. Most people would be angry about the money. But you've never been like that.'"

He laughed. It wasn't a pleasant sound.

"I sat there and smiled. Told you I was proud of you."

"You could have said something." Richard's voice cracked. "You could have told me—"

"Told you what? That I'd spent twenty years waiting for something you were never going to give me?" Danny's voice rose, just slightly. Then he caught himself. Smoothed it back down. "You never asked, Richard. Not once. You just assumed I was happy to serve."

Richard opened his mouth. Closed it. Opened it again.

"That's not—I didn't think of it as—"

"I know you didn't. That's the problem."

The train swayed. Outside, suburbs. Roads. The ordinary architecture of lives that had nothing to do with this room.

Iris thought about the tea in the observation car. The honey Danny had stirred into her cup. The way he'd smiled at her, warm and easy, while she'd sat there not drinking it.

She'd liked him. That was the thing she couldn't get past.

She'd actually liked him.

"And Theo," she said. "They arrested him."

Danny's expression didn't change. "He was useful."

"He's innocent."

"He was never going to walk away clean."

"You'd have let him go to prison."

Danny didn't answer. Which was an answer.

"You figured it out," he said instead. "The flowers, the champagne. How?"

"Mrs. Winslow."

Danny blinked.

"The old woman with the stories about her husband?"

"She's a gardener. She recognized the description."

He laughed—a real laugh this time, startled and bitter.

"I thought about everything. Every detail." He shook his head. "I didn't think about a seventy-year-old woman who knows her flowers."

"You didn't think about Victoria either."

The laugh died.

"No," he said quietly. "I didn't think about Victoria."

Silence.

"She wasn't supposed to be there. At the toast. But she came back. And she grabbed—"

He stopped. His jaw tightened.

"I watched her drink it."

He didn't say anything else. He didn't have to.

Richard stood up suddenly. His face had changed—grief giving way to something harder.

"Twenty years," he said. "Twenty years I loved you. I paid for your education. I held your hand at your mother's funeral. I sat with you every night for a year because you couldn't sleep." His voice was shaking now. "And this is what I get?"

"Richard—"

"No." Richard's hand cut through the air. "You don't get to explain. You don't get to make me understand. A woman is dead. You were going to let an innocent man go to prison. You were going to—"

He couldn't finish.

"Kill you," Danny said quietly. "You can say it."

"I can't." Richard's voice broke. "I can't say it."

The train began to slow. Iris felt it in her bones.

Danny turned toward the window. The platform sliding into view. People waiting. Travelers.

And—standing apart in a way that had nothing to do with patience—uniforms.

Elena, Iris thought. She'd found someone who would listen.

Danny watched them for a long moment.

"Your cabin," he said, still looking out the window. "I searched it. That second night. Looking for any details you might have written about the flower arrangement."

Iris thought about her journal on the desk. The drawers not quite right.

"I read your journal." He glanced at her. "You're observant. But you were looking at the wrong people."

She had been. She'd been so proud of her observations. Sorting everyone into genres like that would keep her safe.

The train hissed to a stop.

Richard was staring at Danny. Grief and rage and love all tangled together.

"Danny." His voice was barely a whisper now. "Please."

Please what, Iris wondered. Please take it back. Please make it not true. Please be the person I thought you were.

Danny didn't answer. There wasn't an answer.

A knock. Loud. Official.

"Deschideți ușa, vă rog." Then, in accented English: "Police. Open the door, please."

Danny straightened his jacket. Unhurried.

"I keep trying to find the moment," he said. "The one where I could have stopped."

He paused.

"I can't find it."

Iris watched him. This man who had taught her about tea. Who had told her about patients he couldn't save. She'd filed him under "devoted nephew." Warm supporting character. The kind who made journeys easier and faded into the background when the story was done.

She'd been wrong.

She kept being wrong about people.

Danny opened the door.

Two officers. Young. Professional.

He held out his hands before they asked. Wrists together.

The handcuffs clicked shut.

They led him into the corridor. Iris moved to the doorway. Richard came with her, unsteady, and she put a hand on his arm without thinking about it.

Danny walked with his head up. Past the other passengers emerging from their cabins—Mrs. Winslow pressing a hand to her chest, Edmund frozen mid-step, faces turning toward something they didn't yet understand.

At the end of the corridor, he paused.

Iris thought he might turn. Say something.

He didn't.

He just kept walking. Onto the platform. Into whatever came next.

They stood there as the train emptied around them. The velvet and brass looked different now. Just furniture. Just a train.

"What do I do now?" Richard asked. His voice was small.

Iris didn't have an answer. Twenty-three years of helping people find things, and she didn't have an answer for this.

"I don't know," she said. "But you don't have to figure it out alone."

She took his arm. The way you guide someone who's forgotten how to walk.

"Come on," she said. "Let's get off this train."

24

The train didn't leave Bucharest for four hours.

There were interviews and statements, the same questions coming at her in different accents and uniforms, some of them tripping over the names of flowers as if that were the strangest part of the story.

As if murder were ordinary, but oleander pronunciation required careful attention."

Iris answered over and over again until it all started to sound less like something she'd lived and more like something she was reciting.

The flowers. The champagne.

The tea she hadn't drunk, which suddenly felt like the most important part.

Yes, she was sure.

Yes, Danny Morrison.

The nephew.

The surgeon.

They gave her coffee in a borrowed office in the station.

Someone had left their family photos on the desk: a woman in a winter coat with her arm around a man, two children smiling at the camera, a golden retriever caught mid-leap. The kind of picture that said *everything is fine here*, whether it was or not. Iris wondered if the person who worked at this desk had any idea their office was being used to process a murder, or if they'd just return Monday morning to find their coffee mug had been borrowed by Interpol.

Iris sat in the narrow chair and folded her hands in her lap. It felt important not to touch anything, though she wasn't sure why. When they finally let her go, it didn't feel like freedom. More like being dismissed. Like a book reshelved after being skimmed but not checked out.

They handed her back her phone and it felt heavier than it should have.

Seventeen missed calls.

Twenty-three texts.

Six voicemails.

All from Robin.

Iris stared at the numbers.

She pressed play.

"Iris. Call me back. Now. I don't care if you're in a tunnel, I don't care if you have to climb onto the roof of the train. Call me back."

The next one was breathless.

"Okay, I called the embassy. I called the train company. I called a man in Venice who kept saying *signore* like it was going to calm me down. If you are dead, Iris, I swear to god—"

The third was quieter. Not calm. Just smaller.

"I found Interpol. I didn't know you could just... find Interpol. They asked me questions. I told them everything. I don't know if it helps. I don't know if any of this helps. Please be alive."

Iris sat very still, suddenly aware of how hard she was holding herself together.

By the time she reached the last voicemail, her hands were shaking. She hadn't noticed when they started.

"I love you," Robin said.

Iris didn't listen to that one twice. She called her back.

Robin answered before the first ring finished.

"Say something."

"I'm here."

A pause—something between a laugh and a breath that hadn't known where to go.

"Okay. Okay. You're here. Where is here?"

"Bucharest. They stopped the train."

"And?"

"They arrested him," Iris said. Her voice sounded steadier than she felt, like something she'd borrowed.

"The nephew?"

"Yes."

Robin exhaled hard. "I didn't know what else to do. I just... kept calling."

"I know," Iris said.

"Did any of it get through?"

"Eventually."

"Eventually," Robin repeated, as if personally offended by the concept. "Are you hurt?"

"No."

"Are you alone?"

"No. Richard's here."

"Okay." Robin sounded like she was pacing. "Okay. When are you coming home?"

"I'm going to finish the trip," Iris said. "I didn't come all of this way just to turn around now."

Iris waited for the pause. For the argument. For the gentle attempt to make her choose safety over momentum.

Robin didn't say *don't*. Robin had never been the person who asked you to shrink back down once you'd finally stood up.

"Of course you are," she said, exhausted. "Because if you went through all that and didn't even get Istanbul, I'd have to murder someone myself."

Iris closed her eyes.

"I don't know what it's going to feel like," Iris admitted. "When I step off. I just know I need to be there. Even now."

"Okay," Robin said. "Then be there. And then come home."

"I will."

"Promise?"

"Promise."

After she hung up, Iris stood in the station hallway for a long moment, staring at nothing. Somewhere down the platform, a cart rattled over uneven stone. A train announcement echoed and died without explanation. She felt briefly grateful that no one was asking her anything.

By the time she boarded again, the train was still sitting at the Bucharest platform, doors open, the delay stretching on as if it might last forever.

Passengers drifted back aboard in small, subdued groups. Staff moved quietly, as if volume itself might cause trouble.

She went to find Richard.

She found him in the observation car, sitting in the same seat where they'd talked earlier in the trip. He wasn't reading. Wasn't looking at the view. Just sitting, hands folded, as if he were waiting for something to finish happening.

She sat down across from him.

"I should have seen it," Richard said finally. His voice was hoarse. "He was always... there."

"Love makes a lot of things look ordinary," Iris said.

Richard closed his eyes. Just for a second.

"Yes," he said. "It does."

They sat like that for a moment, the train noises filling the space between them.

Outside, luggage was being loaded onto the platform. A child was crying. Somewhere nearby, life was resuming whether anyone was ready or not.

"I'll still sign the foundation papers," Richard said after a moment. "That hasn't changed. Eleanor would have wanted—" He stopped, then shook his head slightly. "Something has to come of this."

"And Danny?"

Richard was quiet for a long moment. His hand rested lightly against his chest, not pressing, just there.

"He'll face what he's done," he said. "I'll make sure he has lawyers. I'll visit, if they let me." He swallowed. "He's still the boy I taught to drive."

"You can love someone and let them face the consequences," Iris said.

"That sounds exhausting."

"It probably is."

The door to the observation car opened, and Elena stood there, hesitant.

"Ms. Quinn? May I speak with you?"

They stepped into the corridor.

"The police told me the accusations against me have been cleared," Elena said quietly. "The theft. Victoria's claims."

The tightness in her shoulders was gone. Iris hadn't realized how much Elena had been carrying until it wasn't there.

"I'm glad."

"I wanted to thank you," Elena said. "For noticing. For asking."

Iris hesitated. She could still see the moment she'd almost looked away instead.

"I almost didn't."

"But you did." Elena met her eyes.

They stood there for a moment, neither speaking.

"Istanbul in six hours," Elena said. "Can I bring you anything?"

"Coffee," Iris said. "Definitely coffee."

Elena nodded and disappeared down the corridor.

The train shuddered, then began to move.

Iris watched Bucharest slide away, gray and ordinary, as if nothing remarkable had happened there at all. No sign that a woman had died. No sign that a man had just lost the person he loved most. No sign that she herself had come terrifyingly close to not making it this far.

The train gathered speed. The rails found their rhythm again.

Six hours to the city she'd written in a blue journal when she was seventeen.

She felt something twisted and uncomfortable rise in her chest—not guilt, exactly, but a kind of shameful wanting. The world had just broken open. Someone was dead. Richard was shattered. And still a small, stubborn part of her wanted marble bathrooms and minarets and the end of the line.

She wanted to arrive.

She wanted the dream she'd paid for.

Even now.

Especially now.

Iris watched the last of the station disappear and tried to imagine the woman she would be when the train finally stopped.

She couldn't.

But she knew she wasn't the woman who had boarded in London.

For now, that felt like enough.

25

Istanbul arrived without ceremony.

Not the sweeping reveal she'd imagined at seventeen. Not minarets rising on cue or music swelling somewhere just out of earshot. The train slowed. The windows filled with platforms and people and signs she couldn't read fast enough. Heat pressed in through the glass—damp and insistent, carrying smells she couldn't name.

Someone down the corridor laughed too loudly. The sound of relief.

Iris stayed seated until the movement stopped completely.

Her legs felt fine. It was everything else she wasn't sure about.

Outside, porters were already moving, efficient and unbothered. Luggage appeared. Doors opened. The world did what it always did—arriving, departing, rearranging itself—whether anyone was ready or not.

When she finally stood, the compartment felt different. Like a room after guests had gone. Everything back where it belonged, but the air still holding what had happened there.

She thought about the woman who had boarded in London.

The one with the tissue paper stuck to her hem. The one who had been so sure she didn't belong.

That woman had worn red and watched a man get slapped and helped catch a murderer.

That woman had almost been poisoned over tea.

She picked up her bag and stepped into the corridor.

The train smelled faintly of coffee and polish and something floral she would always associate now with danger. She walked slowly, not because she was unsteady, but because she didn't want to hurry the last stretch of it.

She passed Danny's cabin. Empty now, stripped of whatever had made it his.

She didn't let herself slow down.

At the door, she stopped.

The platform was right there. Three steps down. Ordinary steps, metal-edged, worn by a century of passengers. She had imagined this moment so many times. In the teenage journal. In the years that followed. In the quiet spaces of her apartment when she let herself want things she'd trained herself not to expect.

She had imagined stepping off transformed. Confident. Finished somehow, the way heroines were finished at the end of their stories.

She didn't feel finished.

She stepped off anyway.

One step. That was all it took. One step, and thirty-three years of someday became now.

Her foot met the platform—solid, ordinary, real. Not marble. Not gold. Just concrete, scuffed by a thousand other arrivals. Istanbul didn't roll out a carpet. Istanbul just let her in.

The heat hit her full in the face. Voices layered over one another in languages she couldn't sort. A call rang out from somewhere she couldn't see—musical and commanding. A call to prayer, she realized. The sound she'd read about in books and never quite believed was real until it moved through her chest.

Somewhere on the platform, a sign said ISTANBUL in block letters, and for a second she had the strange, hollow feeling of seeing a word she'd carried in her head for decades suddenly become a place you could step onto. A place with pigeons and trash cans and a man selling something from a cart.

Thirty-three years, she thought. And it was just here. Being Istanbul. Not caring whether I showed up or not.

There was something almost offensive about that.

And something freeing.

Richard was behind her. Leaning more heavily on his cane than usual, but upright. He looked thinner. Older. Still himself.

"Well," he said. "We made it."

"We did."

They stood side by side for a moment. Two people who had survived something together and didn't yet know what it meant.

"I keep doing that," Richard said quietly. "Thinking about what he would have said. What he would have noticed."

"The habit," Iris said. "That doesn't go away quickly."

"No." His voice was rough. "I suppose it doesn't."

A porter approached, and then someone was telling them where to go next, and the moment passed the way moments did.

THE HOTEL WAS NOT THE ONE FROM HER TEENAGE IMAGINATION.

That one had been vaguely palatial, staffed by people who existed only to make her feel glamorous. This one was quieter. More practical. A place that didn't expect anything from you.

Iris was grateful for that.

She checked in. Rode the elevator. Found her room.

The door closed behind her with a soft click.

She stood there for a moment. Not moving. Not thinking. Just letting the silence settle.

The room was clean and quiet and completely indifferent to what she'd been through to get here. It didn't know about the champagne or the flowers or the man who'd tried to poison her over tea. It was just a room. Waiting to be slept in. Waiting to be left.

For the first time in days, no one was watching. No one was waiting. No one needed her to notice anything or explain anything or survive anything.

She was just here. Alone. In Istanbul.

She crossed to the window and pushed it open.

The city rose below her, and for a moment she forgot to breathe.

Not because it was grand. It wasn't—not from here. No postcard angles. No famous silhouettes. Just roofs and balconies, stone and water, light catching where it could. A woman was hanging laundry on a line, white sheets bellying in the breeze. A man was arguing into a phone, one hand cutting the air for emphasis. A cat picked its way along a wall with the confidence of something that owned every surface it touched.

Ordinary. All of it ordinary.

And somehow that was the thing that undid her.

She had spent thirty-three years imagining something extraordinary. Something that would justify the waiting. The wanting. The decades of someday.

But this was just a city. Just people doing their laundry and arguing on phones and going about their lives. Just a place that had been here the whole time, not waiting for her at all.

She had thought she needed to earn this. To become someone who deserved it first. Someone thinner or braver or more interesting. Someone who wore silk and knew what to do with a cheese course.

She had been wrong.

She just had to show up.

Fable would approve, she thought. Fable had always just shown up. Had never once wondered if she deserved the sunny spot on the couch.

Her phone vibrated.

Robin: *Did you get there? Are you dead? Send proof of life immediately.*

Iris smiled.

Alive. In Istanbul. Looking at rooftops and laundry and a very confident cat.

Robin: *Proof of life accepted. How does it feel?*

Iris thought about it.

Like finishing a book and not knowing what to read next.

Robin: *That's either very profound or you need sleep.*

Probably both.

Robin: *Go look at something beautiful. Then call me. I want to hear all of it.*

Tomorrow. I promise.

Robin: *And Iris?*

Yes?

Robin: *You did it. Whatever else happened—you did the thing. The seventeen-year-old is extremely smug right now.*

Iris set the phone down. Her eyes were stinging.

She let them.

LATER, SHE WENT OUT.

Down on the street, the city met her without interest. A shopkeeper nodded. A woman argued cheerfully into her phone. A different cat—same proprietary air—slept in the shade of an awning.

She walked without a destination, letting the streets decide.

Past a mosque with tourists clustered at its entrance. Past a man selling roasted chestnuts from a cart. Past a bookshop with volumes in a dozen languages spilling onto tables outside.

She stopped at the bookshop. Of course she did.

The owner looked up, assessed her with the quick efficiency of someone who had seen ten thousand tourists, and returned to his newspaper. She was not interesting. She was just another person looking at books.

That was fine. Books could take care of themselves.

She found a volume of Turkish poetry with facing translations. Found a history of the city with illustrations that made her want to sit down immediately.

Found, to her surprise, a battered English paperback of *Murder on the Orient Express*.

She laughed out loud.

The shopkeeper glanced up.

She bought the poetry and the history. Left the Christie where it was. She had lived that story now. She didn't need to read it anymore.

SHE FOUND A CAFÉ THAT LOOKED LIKE IT HAD BEEN THERE FOR A HUNDRED years and would be there for a hundred more. She ordered something she couldn't pronounce, pointing at the menu and trusting the result. The waiter brought coffee in a small copper pot, thick and dark, with a glass of water and a single piece of something sweet on a tiny plate.

She drank it slowly. Let the bitterness settle on her tongue.

She thought about all the tea Danny had tried to teach her to love.

I'm still a coffee person, she thought. I'm always going to be a coffee person.

Some things didn't change. That was all right too.

By the water, in the long golden hour before sunset, Iris found a bench and sat.

The light was doing something she'd never seen before. Copper and rose and something almost violet, layering over the water like veils being drawn back one at a time. The city on the far shore had gone soft-edged, its outlines dissolving into the haze. A gull hung motionless in the air above her, wings tilted, riding a current she couldn't feel.

She watched it.

Such a small thing. A bird doing what birds did. But it stayed there, suspended, as if the whole world had paused to let her look.

The city went on around her—voices, engines, footsteps, the soft slap of water against stone, another call to prayer rising and falling like breath.

A ferry passed, crowded with commuters heading home. A man on the deck raised his hand to someone on the shore.

An ordinary gesture. An ordinary day. For everyone except her.

She thought about the woman who had clicked "confirm" in her apartment three weeks ago. The one who had been so afraid. So sure she was making a mistake. So ready for the universe to intervene and stop her.

The universe hadn't stopped her.

And now she was here. In the city she'd written in a journal at seventeen. Watching light move over water. Listening to a language she didn't speak. Smelling something on the wind—salt and exhaust and roasting meat and something sweet she couldn't name.

She had wanted this for so long.

She had wanted it so badly she'd stopped believing she could have it.

And now it was here. Not perfect. Not the dream exactly. But real.

Real was better.

Something released in her chest. Not dramatic. Not a sob. Just a loosening, like a knot she'd been holding so long she'd forgotten it was there.

She sat with it. Let it move through her.

When it passed, she felt lighter. Not fixed. Not finished. Just lighter.

She didn't take out her phone.

Didn't reach for her journal.

Didn't try to decide what it meant or what genre it belonged to.

She just stayed.

In Istanbul.

The word she had carried for thirty-three years, now a place with wind and noise and uneven pavement under her feet and the taste of bitter coffee still on her tongue.

After a while, after the gull had moved on and the light had shifted from gold to pink to something approaching violet, she stood.

She walked back into the city.

Not toward the hotel. Not yet.

Just further in. Deeper.

The way you went deeper into a book when you weren't ready for it to end.

26

The apartment was exactly the same.

That was the first thing Iris noticed when she unlocked the door and stepped inside, dragging her suitcase over the familiar threshold. Same beige walls she'd been meaning to paint for six years. Same sofa cushions molded to her particular way of sitting. Same faint smell of coffee and dust and the neighbor's laundry detergent drifting in through the vents. The fern by the window was still alive. Better than she'd left it, thanks to Robin.

Fable looked up from the arm of the couch. She blinked once, slowly, in the manner of someone acknowledging a delay that had been inconvenient but survivable.

"I'm home," Iris said.

Fable yawned. Her teeth were very small and very white and completely indifferent to transcontinental travel.

Fair enough.

Iris set her suitcase by the door and stood there longer than necessary, keys still in her hand. The silence felt different now.

Not better. Just... changed. Like a room after furniture had been moved and put back again. Familiar, but slightly misaligned.

She kicked off her shoes. One landed on its side. She nudged it straight with her toe, then immediately nudged it crooked again, annoyed at herself for caring.

A week ago, she would have lined them up without thinking. Toes forward. Entropy held at bay. Now she could look at the crooked shoe and leave it there. Progress.

Fable flicked an ear. Judgment, possibly. Or just a draft.

She made coffee. Poured it into her chipped blue mug, the one that said READ BANNED BOOKS, and leaned against the counter while the machine clicked itself quiet.

The trip had ended.

That part was over.

The train. The mountains. The noise. The death.

She waited for the letdown. The crash. The sense that she'd briefly lived someone else's life and was now back where she belonged. She'd read about this. Post-travel depression, the articles called it. The return to ordinary life after extraordinary experience. The inevitable diminishment.

It didn't come.

Instead, there was just... quiet. And coffee. And a cat who had never once, in her entire life, wondered if she belonged anywhere.

Her phone vibrated against the counter.

Robin: *So. How does it feel to be not dead?*

Iris huffed a laugh before she could stop herself.

Iris: *Disappointingly ordinary. No dramatic afterglow.*

Robin: *Rude. I was hoping for at least one personality change.*

Iris: *Sorry to disappoint. Still me.*

A pause.

Robin: *You home?*

Iris: *Yeah. Fable is pretending she didn't notice I was gone.*

Robin: *Classic Fable. Give her a chin scratch from me. She'll hate it.*

Iris: *Done.*

Robin: *I called Interpol, you know. While you were off solving murders.*

Iris: *I'm aware. You told me. Also, I listened to your voicemails.*

Robin: *The one where I yelled at a man in Venice was a particular highlight.*

Iris: *He didn't deserve that.*

Robin: *He kept saying "signora" like it would calm me down. He absolutely deserved it. We'll debrief properly tomorrow. When you've slept. Or stared at the ceiling long enough to give up.*

Iris: *I missed you.*

Three dots appeared. Disappeared. Appeared again.

Robin: *I know. Welcome back.*

The phone went still again.

Iris set it face down and immediately turned it face up again, just in case.

Later, because time had lost some of its urgency somewhere between Istanbul and Logan Airport, Iris unpacked.

Like unpacking on the Orient Express, this also took approximately seven minutes.

Laundry in one pile. Shoes in another. A book she'd bought at the airport and forgotten about. It was heavy, glossy, the kind of impulse purchase that made no sense until it did. She set that on the counter to deal with later.

The red dress hung back in the closet. No more tissue paper.

The first night on the train, she'd had tissue paper stuck to her hem. Mrs. Winslow had pointed it out, matter-of-fact, while explaining something about Herbert's theories on proper documentation. That felt like months ago. That felt like another woman entirely.

The dress looked different now. Like it was hers.

She closed the closet door and stood there for a moment, listening to the apartment settle.

Fable had migrated to the bedroom doorway, watching with the air of a supervisor who found the work adequate but uninspired.

Iris sat down at the small kitchen table and opened her journal.

She stared at the blank page longer than she'd meant to.

What did you write after something like that? After murder and survival and the slow understanding that waiting wasn't the same as preparing, that someday wasn't a promise but an evasion?

She didn't try to answer.

Instead, she wrote:

Home again. Fable unimpressed. The kettle still squeaks.

That felt right.

She added:

I don't know what comes next.

She left that one.

She closed the journal. Opened it again. Added, smaller beneath the last line:

That's probably okay.

She capped the pen, then uncapped it, then capped it again, annoyed at herself.

The book was still on the counter. She picked it up, heavier than she remembered.

The Last Great Ocean Liners.

She sat back down and flipped it open.

Black-and-white photographs. Long decks. Women in hats leaning against railings, gazing at nothing in particular. Ships built for crossings, not efficiency. Vessels that took their time getting anywhere.

She turned pages. The *Normandie*. The *United States*. The original *Queen Mary*, retired now to a California harbor. Beautiful things, all of them gone or diminished. Turned into museums or memories or rust.

And then, near the end, in color: the *Queen Mary 2*.

She stopped.

The photograph showed her at sea, cutting through gray Atlantic water, red and black funnel bright against an overcast sky. Not a relic. Not a memory. A working ship, still crossing, still carrying people between the old world and the new.

She read a page. Then another.

Days at sea. Formal dinners with nowhere else to go. A library —the largest at sea, the book said, with thousands of volumes. Lectures by authors and historians. Reading rooms with actual armchairs.

The largest library at sea.

Iris read that sentence twice. Seven thousand books, apparently, and seven days to read them.

She turned the page slowly.

Of course, she thought. *Of course that exists.*

There was a strange intimacy in the idea of being carried forward without being able to rush the ending.

A week, the book said. Seven days between New York and Southampton. No ports. No distractions. Just the ship and the sea and whatever you brought with you.

She thought about the Orient Express. The speed of it. Mountains appearing and disappearing. Cities announced and then gone. The constant forward motion, no time to catch her breath, no room to sit with what was happening.

She thought about Richard in the observation car at two in the morning, talking about Tuscany. *We never went. There was always a reason.* There was always going to be time later. Until there wasn't.

Seven days was a long time. Seven days was nothing. It

depended entirely on whether you were spending them or saving them.

Iris looked up from the page.

Fable had migrated to the table and was watching her with the intensity of a cat who suspected dinner was being delayed for frivolous reasons.

"It's not the same thing," Iris said. "A crossing isn't a train. And it's not that expensive."

Fable's tail twitched.

She turned another page. A photograph of the grand lobby, all Art Deco lines and warm light. A shot of the Commodore Club, passengers in evening dress holding cocktails, the windows nothing but black and stars.

She thought about the Orient Express. How it had felt like stepping into someone else's story. A story that moved too fast, that demanded she keep up.

This looked different. This looked like a story you could wander through. One that gave you room to think.

She closed the book and set it beside her journal, the two of them touching at the corners like they belonged to the same conversation.

That evening, Iris stood at the window and watched Boston do what Boston always did. Rush. Honk. Someone walked a dog in a crocheted sweater. A bus hissed past.

Some things were stubbornly consistent.

She picked up her phone.

Her bank app icon sat in the corner of the screen, patient and unblinking. She hadn't opened it since before the trip. Hadn't wanted to see what remained after forty-eight thousand dollars had been converted into train tickets and attempted murder and that one perfect cup of coffee in Istanbul.

She still didn't open it.

Schrödinger's bank account. As long as she didn't look, she

both had savings and didn't have savings. The balance existed in a quantum state of maybe-fine and probably-alarming.

She opened her browser instead.

Just to look, she told herself.

She was very good at looking.

Queen Mary 2. Transatlantic Crossing. New York to Southampton.

Seven nights. Departing New York.

She thought about the seventeen-year-old who had wanted this. Not the crossing specifically—she hadn't known about crossings then—but the wanting. The sense that the world was larger than the life she'd been handed, and that someday she would find a way to see it.

That girl had waited thirty-three years.

She'd been right to wait, Iris had told herself. She'd been sensible. Practical. Responsible.

She'd also been wrong.

Iris scrolled. Staterooms. Deck plans. Prices that made her wince, then prices that made her pause.

"I'm not booking anything," Iris told the room.

Fable jumped onto the table and sat squarely on the journal.

"I'm just looking. There's a difference."

Iris scrolled down. Found the sailing schedule. Found a date in spring—April, when Boston would still be gray but the Atlantic would be starting to warm.

She didn't click on it.

She just looked at it for a long time.

The largest library at sea.

She closed the laptop.

Not as a refusal.

As a bookmark.

The closet door was three steps away. She opened it again.

She dug through, found her leather notebook. The expensive

one, the kind real writers used. *Chapter One* on the first page in her best handwriting. Nothing after. She'd bought it at thirty-two, certain she had a novel in her.

She pulled it out. Turned past that hopeful first page to a blank one.

No One Sleeps on the Orient Express

She didn't know yet if it was a novel or a memoir or just a very long letter to the woman she used to be.

She kept writing anyway.

BOOK CLUB GUIDE

Because every mystery is better with good company and snacks.

You don't need a luxury train car to host a great book discussion. Just a few thoughtful touches and the willingness to lean into the cozy.

Atmosphere

Create a setting that feels warm, welcoming, and just a little bit glamorous. The kind of place Iris would absolutely sit and listen. Soft lamp-light rather than overheads. Instrumental jazz or classical music turned low. A scarf or throw in midnight blue, wine-red, or emerald. A small vase of white flowers (a quiet nod to the story, without spoilers). Encourage sweaters. No one should solve mysteries while chilly.

Menu Ideas

Savory: Finger sandwiches (cucumber, smoked salmon, or chicken salad), a simple cheese board with crackers, nuts, and dried fruit, mini quiches or spanakopita. *Sweet:* Petit fours or macarons, shortbread cookies, anything that belongs on a tiered tea tray. *Drinks:* Champagne or sparkling cider for a "midnight toast," a selection of teas (Earl Grey, English Breakfast, chamomile), coffee for those who, like Iris, will always quietly prefer it. Store-bought is completely acceptable. No one is grading your pastry skills.

Icebreaker

Start with something light: *What is your "someday trip," and what has kept you from booking it (so far)?* Answers may range from "Paris" to "anywhere with room service," and all are correct.

Suggested Discussion Flow

If you like a bit of structure (Iris would approve): Start with characters. Who surprised you? Who frustrated you? Then the mystery. When did you first suspect something deeper was wrong? Move to themes: belonging, reinvention, permission, and midlife bravery. Discuss the ending. What satisfied you? What would you have done differently? And finally, what's next for Iris? If she boarded another train, where should it go?

Optional Extras

A bookmark swap where everyone brings a favorite to trade. A detective round: who did you suspect, and when did you change your mind? A travel jar where guests write down dream destinations, then draw and discuss one at the end. Magnifying glasses optional, but highly encouraged if you already own one.

A Closing Toast

To second chances, to trips we haven't taken yet, and to books that let us go anyway.

Thank you for choosing to read and discuss this story. Iris would be quietly delighted to ride along to your next meeting.

DISCUSSION QUESTIONS

1. Iris spends years saying "someday." What finally pushes her to act? Have you ever had a "someday" that turned into now?

2. The Orient Express represents luxury, escape, and reinvention. What did the train symbolize for Iris, and did that symbolism change after the murder?

3. Which scene first made you think something was truly wrong? What detail tipped you off?

4. Iris often catalogues people by "genre." Did you recognize anyone in your own life in those descriptions, or in Iris herself?

5. The book plays with the idea of who belongs somewhere. Who on the train felt most out of place to you, and why?

6. Several characters perform versions of themselves for status, safety, or survival. Whose performance was the most convincing, and whose cracked first?

7. Iris isn't a detective. She's a librarian. How do her skills shape the investigation differently than a traditional sleuth's would?

8. What did you think about Victoria before and after her death? Did your feelings toward her shift?

9. The night of chaos on the train is both funny and unsettling. Where did you feel the line between humor and danger, and how did the book balance both?

10. Who did you suspect at different points, and what misled you? Did the story "play fair" with clues?

11. Several characters carry quiet grief, regrets, or secrets. Which one affected you most, and why?

12. Friendship plays a subtle role, especially between Iris and Robin. How does Robin shape Iris's choices, even from afar?

13. The theme of permission runs throughout the book: permission to travel, want things, take up space. Where did you see Iris finally stop asking for permission?

14. If you could ask one character a question they never answered in the book, who would it be, and what would you ask?

15. Imagine the story from another character's point of view: Elena, Theo, Margaret. How would the mystery, or Iris, look different?

16. Cozy mysteries promise comfort despite danger. What felt "cozy" to you in this book, and what intentionally broke that feeling?

17. What do you think Iris takes home from this journey, besides the story? How might her life change afterward?

18. And finally: If you could take any dream trip (murder-free), where would you go, and what's been stopping you?

www.ingramcontent.com/pod-product-compliance
Lightning Source LLC
Chambersburg PA
CBHW020936310726
48980CB00007B/797/J

* 9 7 9 8 9 9 9 6 8 9 3 1 3 *